Feather

in a

Gaslamp

Steven Paul Watson

For Dad.

The Ulysses Journey

Book One

Prologue

Mia landed awkwardly, with the air knocked from her body. Everything ached from the impact on the unforgiving ground. She heard someone speak but couldn't make out what he was saying the first go around for the ringing in her ears. She couldn't understand why someone was speaking some form of garbled language that she couldn't comprehend. And Mia, though young, already spoke three languages.

"Stay down." It came more clearly to her once her ears quit blasting the echo of the crowd and her own heartbeat lodged in her throat. "Stay down." She scrambled forward on her belly until she picked up the smooth rock in the palm of her hand. "Stay down," he repeated as she took a deep breath and sat up on her knees. She looked at the crowd around her as she slowly crept back to her bare feet.

"Stay down." This last time sounded like her own voice somewhere in the back of her mind.

Mia would not stay down. It was one thing her mother, above all, had taught her. Don't back down, and if you get knocked down, always get back up. No matter how difficult the obstacle may seem, get back up.

She balled her hand up into a tight fist encircling a smooth, surfaced stone. Her ribs ached. She hadn't even felt the pain until she stumbled around to face the boy who had knocked her down so violently. She clenched her jaw tightly. She could feel the inside of her palm ache; it would no doubt be bruised from the stone.

"Don't," the boy said, his eyes narrowing, knowing she wasn't going to stop. His lips parted into a partial smile. He didn't want her to stop. He wanted to beat the outsider. His expression changed as she wiped the blood from her chin. It flowed freely from her mouth now, causing her to grit her teeth, tasting the blood in the back of her throat. Mia smiled, leaping, letting her rage carry her twice as far as she'd thought possible into the much larger boy.

She was breathing so heavily through her nose that she wasn't sure if she could do anything but hear the rumble of her own heart beating in her chest. She almost didn't hear them. The other children around cheered and screamed at the chaos they'd witnessed. The other girls cheered her on. She didn't quite understand why they were cheering for her now when most days they gossiped and called her names behind her back. Because of who her father and mother were, she was going to always be an outsider no matter where she tried to call home. She stood wiping the blood from her mouth again and glared down at the red on her knuckles and the boy at her feet with his busted lip and a broken nose, a long gash on his cheek that would no doubt scar. He was two years older than her and had tormented her from the moment she had arrived by calling her names, making every waking moment something dreaded, all because she was different. She clenched her hands into a fist, ignoring the ache in the hand that held the stone.

He moved faster than she expected, kicking her legs out from under her and buckling her knees until she was nearly eye level with him. He smiled, his teeth bloodied as it ran out from the crease in his mouth. He went for her abdomen with his left hand, and she smacked it away as his left punched her in the middle of her stomach. She fell backward, wheezing and staring up at the sky. The cheers had died down as she rolled over, got to her feet, and stared back at him just as he pulled himself up to a standing position of his own. She charged, a blur of anger and pain. She had toppled him like he was a toddler, using his weight against him. Her hand ached from the first punch; it had gone numb after not realizing just how many times she had struck him.

It wasn't the first time she had dealt with a bully. In Boston, it was much the same because of her Cherokee heritage. And here she was with her father's people… again standing over a boy twice her size with his blood on her balled-up fist. She knew he should stay down, but he wouldn't. The boy in Boston didn't stay down, either. They could not let a girl beat them, always with the same motivation, no matter the cost.

In a couple of years, this boy at her feet struggling to get back up would be allowed to go out on hunts with the other young men. He could not be beaten by a girl now; he would never live down the embarrassment. And he especially could not let an outsider beat him. She could see him, filled with embarrassment and anger. He reached his feet, wiping the blood from his face. It did little more than smear it like war paint across his tanned skin. The boys around them didn't cheer, but they yelled at him, encouraging him to hurt her and feeding his rage. A fury she could see bubbling up inside of him as he narrowed his eyes, and his neck pulsated. He didn't smile. She could see his muscles as they tense. His jaw clenched just before he acted.

He charged, but she dodged. His blind rage made it easy for him to dodge with ease. The cheering roared even louder as he slid face-first into the mud. She laughed. She didn't mean to. She even placed her bruised hand over her mouth, seeing him swiftly roll onto his back. It only enraged him more. Quick to his feet, he roared, unable to form words.

"You don't have to do this," she muttered, but she could see it in his eyes, he did. Again, he charged. This time, she could not dodge as he tackled her to the ground. But when the tumbling stopped, despite her smaller size, she was the one on top. They never learned that size wasn't always an advantage. With his arms pinned to the ground under her knees. She smiled.

It was then they heard the laughter of others, adults. She looked to see her father standing watch over the rambunctious activities. She looked down at her opponent, his face turned away from her, prepared for a repeat of the onslaught she'd given him the first time around. She almost felt sorry for him before she looked at her father again. Her father stood with his arms crossed against his thick chest; his expression was blank, but she knew what the blank canvas meant. He was angry.

"Come with me, daughter," he said, maintaining his stoic expression. To anyone who looked at them, he didn't seem disappointed or happy with what the entirety of the village had just witnessed. But she could hear it in his voice and only the small wrinkle of his brow she was sure no one else noticed. She quickly went to her feet, feeling the boy move the moment her weight was gone. She could even hear him sob under what had just happened. She rushed to reach her father's side, keeping her head lowered and eyes away from him. She wished she could have gone back in time and stopped the fight before it happened, all so she didn't have to face her father's wrath.

She knew she was in trouble. It was not her duty, the activities of the boys. And to embarrass him would also not be looked upon as anything but a disappointment. She followed suit, a mile, then two, then the third mile, and she began to feel a tinge of anxiety.

Where was her father leading her?

"Where are we going?" It came from her involuntarily. She had not meant to say it aloud. Her father never slowed his stride. He just looked back at her with a love-filled smile. "Are you going to send me back to Boston?" she muttered. He stopped in his tracks at those words. He never looked back at her but glanced at the crows in the nearby trees before they flew away. She had lost track of how far they had walked, but the sun had dropped from the sky, and the moon was starting to climb when she saw something clearly in the light coming from a fire. She hesitated, and he heard her.

Her father turned and spoke, "Come, we are almost there, daughter." Her father, who always had such a stern, neutral tone with everyone, including her, almost sounded sad when he spoke now.

"He is going to send you back to Boston," that voice in the back of her head growled.

Mia's stomach grumbled, and she felt a tremble in her legs before she stepped forward, following through the narrow trail until she realized the fire was getting bigger and bigger as they emerged into the clearing. "Who is that...?"

"A shaman, daughter," he replied, turning to face her. "I want you to go to him. Listen to him, but all that he tells you is for you and the stars and flames alone to hear. You must never tell anyone what it is he tells you."

She watched her father move with hesitation. She thought she could see the ancestors of old on his shoulders, encouraging him to move away from her until he was gone. Mia turned slowly, giving another look back to where her father had disappeared into the wilderness under the cover of smoke before she approached the other man. His appearance alone scared her. He was naked except for his loincloth and the wolf cap on his head. The wolf's eyes followed her with every step she took, but she still continued to press on. Just like the boy in camp and the one in Boston, she would not let the fear she was feeling control her.

The shaman took her hands, observing her bloodied knuckles, and twisted her palm to look at the freshly formed bruise. She saw the reflection of her smile in his eyes. She hadn't even realized she was smiling as she looked down. His lips never twitched from his cold frown. "The young she-wolf, the stars have brought you to me." He turned her hand around as she unfolded her fist. She never saw the knife as he cut her already sore, bruised palm. She grimaced but did not pull away as the blood slowly bubbled from the cut. He took his thumb and marked her face with three smears of her own blood. One was on the forehead, and one was on each cheek, and then he marked his face the same. "Sit." She folded her feet under her, sitting across from him. He turned for a moment, looking at the flames, and then looked again at the stars above. He kept this up for what felt like an eternity. She had lost track of time as he repeated the pattern over and over and over, to the point where her lips quivered with words she couldn't say. Even thinking about them left her feeling uneasy.

"Such a troubled future, death, love, so much loss, I see a life I don't... I don't understand," he said. His voice broke her from her daze, and she realized the moon had nearly crossed the sky above them. She could see his expression but couldn't understand it. There was a mix of fear and wonderment.

Mia didn't understand how so much time had passed. The moon was already falling, when it had still been day when she'd been left at the stranger's fire. Hours had passed since she arrived. She started to talk, but he placed a finger on her lip without even looking. "The life of a warrior, a wife, and the young she-wolf will see things I still do not believe are possible though I have seen it with my own eyes. I see blood falling like rain on a white man's city, and you are responsible for the letting. I see you in love… and being loved by someone not your own… I see you fighting side by side with a sworn enemy… Protecting a young girl from a demon… All I have seen, I believe, but I do not know how any of this is possible." The shaman broke from his routine. His face still showed the same expression. "Go, join your father." She quickly did as the shaman said.

Chapter One

November 1876

Mia opened her eyes. She could almost see the reflection of her father's smile in the window. It had been a couple of years since he had passed away and twice as long since she'd last seen him. She still had his letters tucked away back at her home. It felt like sometimes it had been a lifetime since she returned to Boston. In a way, it was. She had spent her youth in two vastly different worlds, both of which came with their own advantages and disadvantages. She often thought about those last few days spent with her father, and the shaman had made it clear that she needed to be with her mother. Or so that was what her father had insisted. Mia clenched her jaw so hard she could feel the pulse in her neck quicken. The memory was a source of scattered emotions for her.

"Are you okay, ma'am?" She glanced over at the little girl who was cradled in her mother's arms, "You look like you're about to cry."

Mia felt it. There, just under the surface, she was about to weep, and the little girl with her curly blond hair stared at her so intently with her innocent eyes.

"I'm fine," she lied, looking up at the girl's mother, who was whispering something to her that Mia couldn't hear over the sound of the train. "Thank you for asking." She leaned forward, putting her hand on the little girl's hand resting on her knee, and the mother pulled the girl closer to her. Mia recoiled, looking at the other woman, and clenched her jaw harder before she looked at her companions. The train lurched as it began to slow at an accelerated pace, sending a shrill screech through the cabin. Mia shifted in her seat and grabbed the stabilizing bar, which held her in a more composed position. She glanced at the woman who had pulled her daughter in tighter, but the little girl's eyes were still glued to her, and she was smiling.

Mia knew they were not in Washington, DC; she had traveled many times from Boston to DC, and it was several hours before they'd be there even now. Mia watched her two companions with the same look of confusion she was certain she reflected. She twisted to pull the dirty teal curtains wider from her window to get a better look. Mia had not even realized it was raining, but she saw the downpour beating against the glass. She was sure it would shatter if the drops hit much harder. It surprised her. She had been looking at the glass lost in old memories, what seemed like only a minute before. Lightning flashed in the distance; the sound of thunder had been masked by the train's engine. She smiled, watching the storm, untamed, as she felt she once was. She turned and heard one of her companions stand. Benson was a large man, and she wasn't sure of his exact age, but she was sure he was in his late fifties. His hair was thinning, and his beard was full of grayer than the natural brown of his youth. He moved with ease to the door, shifting his coat over his firearm in a swift motion with his hand on the handle of his Colt. He did not pull his weapon, but she had seen him do so often in practice and knew how deadly accurate he was from his hip. This made her uncomfortable. If Benson felt there was reason to be armed, she unclenched her jaw, wanting to reach for her small one-shot pistol hidden away in her bustle.

"I'm sure it is nothing," her other companion spoke up. Jean was Benson's daughter, though Mia often wondered if it was true as there were no similarities between the two in appearance. Though she had heard her husband say that Jean was the "spitting image" of the girl's mother, a woman whom

Mia had never met and couldn't recall her name. Mia watched the older man glance back to his only child and then to the door as he cracked it open to get a better look out into the hall. Mia didn't speak. It wasn't her place to question. Benson had been her guardian with her husband, Logan, away. She had relied on him more than she wanted to admit, and when the letter came asking for her to visit Washington, it was Benson from whom she had sought advice. She glanced back to the outside, seeing equestrians pass by the window at an excessive pace toward the front of the train. There were at least six riders moving at a dangerous pace, considering the darkness and rain. She watched until they were out of sight.

"There are riders boarding the train," Mia let the curtain shut and started to stand, getting a look back from Benson. She watched the mother and daughter, who no longer paid her any mind but kept their eyes on the behemoth of a man standing in the doorway. She unclipped the top of her blouse, giving her easier access to the derringer 22 if she needed it. It was only a single shot gun, and she now wished she had access to her revolvers hidden away in her luggage compartment. Even if she wasn't as good as Benson at quick draw, she was still an adequate shot when she had the opportunity to aim.

Mia turned, hearing Benson step from the door. He was to the window in a blink of an eye before turning away, looking from one woman to the next before returning to the door. "What is it, Papa?" She could hear the commotion coming from somewhere outside. The six men were searching the train.

"Something isn't right…" She saw his worry-filled eyes as he took another peek out the door and quickly closed it. Mia didn't have to see it for herself; she could hear footsteps coming down the hall, and it was only a moment before the knock startling her as she rested a hand across her collar, ready to pull her only weapon. "Mrs. Mia Ezekiel?"

"Who asks?" Benson stepped back from the door, pulling his pistol, keeping his body between her and the door. She'd admit, Benson looked intimidating. She never doubted the man's loyalty to her husband, but to her, there had been times, especially since Logan's disappearance, when she wondered.

The door crept open. She saw the tension in Benson's forearm and half expected him to raise his gun to fire as the man stepped into the opening. But his hand went limp when the large, bearded man stepped further into the light. Mia could see both through a mirror located just within the door, and there was a familiarity there even if she'd never met the intruder. "Hamilton Bastion," the man stated, his voice was deep and grave.

Mia stood up straight, fixed the button on the top of her blouse, and straightened the wrinkles as she looked at the little girl and her mother, who had shrieked at the wall and were almost hidden behind her dress. She gave the girl a wink and the mother a nod and spoke softly, "It's going to be okay." The entirety of the cabin stood in silence as she made herself presentable. Benson kept her hidden, looked over his shoulder at her, and waited for Mia's nod before he stepped to one side.

"Sorry, Mr. Bastion, I didn't realize…" Mia watched Benson place his gun back in its holster. Benson showed mannerisms she had never seen before, not that she could see his face clearer. He almost seemed like he was afraid of Hamilton. He slinked backward a couple of steps and stood with his back to the wall, his eyes lowered. Benson was a bigger man, and it was obvious from looking at the two in much better physical condition, but still, he seemed to shy away.

Mia had never met Hamilton but had met this man's two brothers on occasion, and the similarities between the three were unmistakable. The man standing before her looked just like the man Logan had described, only older and a little heavier. It had been Hamilton Bastion who invited her to visit

Washington. He was nearly sixty, she thought, much older than her or Logan. His wavy hair was more gray than black, and his beard was completely gray. He wore a jacket that she could tell was tailored to his size, and everything down to his pocket watch chain looked like it was freshly shined. She had known Hamilton was wealthy. She'd met his brothers and knew some of their family history, but seeing him for herself was a different story.

"It's quite all right, Benson. You had no way of knowing it was me," Hamilton stated. His voice was smoother now, less aggressive than his introduction. Hamilton smiled as he looked at the other man, who seemed to shrivel almost from sight under his gaze. "But if you would not mind, I would like to speak to Mrs. Ezekiel in private," he said. She was surprised to see Benson move so quickly, nervously. He circled away from the other gentleman, pulling his daughter along roughly with him out of the room. She had never seen Benson so much as raise his voice to Jean, let alone handle her as hard as she had just seen.

She watched as the man pulled a change purse from an upper pocket, plucked some coins free, and held them out to the woman behind Mia. "Go buy your child a chocolate," he said. It was easy to tell the man was looking at the little girl and not the mother. It was the little girl who took the money from his hand.

"Thank you, mister," the mother said as she ushered her daughter from the room without hesitation, much like Benson had made Jean leave the cabin. It was easy to see that Hamilton liked children, and he never stopped watching the little girl until she was gone.

Hamilton's smile leveled on her as the door shut. Mia gathered herself, taking a deep breath. There had always been that presumption about why she was here. She took a seat, watching him take his own across from her, unbuttoning his jacket in the movement. "Do not take offense, Mrs. Ezekiel. You are every bit as beautiful as your husband said you were and more. I feared he had exaggerated, but now I see you with my own eyes. I can only hope my eyes are not deceiving me."

"Is Logan dead?" Mia fidgeted in her seat, afraid of the answer, as the man's eyes lay coldly on her. She had blurted it out so grimly and to the point that she had found she already knew the answer and could not bring herself to meet the man's gaze.

"No, ma'am, your husband is not," Hamilton replied. Mia sighed in relief, not hearing what she'd expected. "I'm sorry if you were living with that presumption this entire train ride down. Maybe I should have been clearer in my letter. My apologies."

Mia found that her heart was no longer racing; she was able to gather her thoughts faster. "Why am I here?" Mia asked now, staring into his eyes. Her bluntness caught him off guard, and he looked toward the darkness, delaying his answer. She could only see some dampness; he must have been wearing a hat and overcoat to remain so dry with the rain outside. "Is my husband in Washington?" She pursued an answer from him now more than ever. She saw his lip quiver with the second question, his face flushed as he turned, looking back to her and leaning forward, reaching out to take her hand in his. Mia quickly pulled away. His touch was cold, but it was more. She could see the sorrow in his eyes. Her stomach quaked, feeling an intense uneasiness. She was not here to be reunited with her estranged husband.

"Both complicated questions," he replied. She could tell he was uncomfortable despite the tailored suit; he fidgeted in his seat; a foot even began to tap in his nervousness, and she could feel the sorrow seep from her body and be replaced with anger.

Mia's agitation grew. "Where is my husband?" She quickly questioned how she knew her voice deepened in its seriousness. "Is Logan here in Washington?" The quiver in his lips worsened. "Forgive my rashness… that is not a complicated question, and you seem hesitant to answer, and it was you who had me brought all this way, so I'm sorry for being blunt, Mister Bastion, but where is my husband?"

"No, I had brought you here to reunite the two of you. It is my fault you've been separated for as long as you have," he replied. "I brought you to Washington because I needed someone I could trust."

"You don't know me," Mia quickly answered. She could feel herself flushed with uncontrollable anger, her hand now resting on the top of her dress again, one finger scratching at her throat, and she could feel the bulk of the Deringer under her palm.

He laughed. But it was not the laughter of joy as he sat back in his seat, "So much truth in your statement. I don't know you, Mia Ezekiel. You see. But I know Logan Ezekiel; he is one of the few people I have ever known who I have trusted completely. His faith and trust in you are why I find myself asking you for your assistance." He again leaned forward, running a hand through his hair. "You see… I am running out of people I trust. You may know me as a stranger, but you, I know all I need to know about you."

"Where is my husband?" Mia leaned forward, mirroring him in her position.

"If you do this one thing for me, Mia, I promise you I will do everything in my power to reunite you with your husband," he quickly replied. She could tell he clenched his jaw in anticipation of her answer.

Mia gritted her teeth, sitting back. She looked away, her reflection in the glass. Now, she could almost feel the chill of the stormy night air as the hair on the back of her neck stood. "What are you asking of me, Mr. Bastion?"

"I need you to take a trip to guardian over my niece until she is back in her mother's arms," he replied. She looked back at him; he was pale, and there was more to what he was asking than simply watching over a young girl. "A girl not so different from the young one who was just here with you in the cabin."

"Why does a little girl need to be watched over?" Mia leaned forward, trying to focus on his eyes, but he wouldn't settle to continue to look anywhere but directly at her.

"These are delicate times. All others who I find I could trust are otherwise engaged, so I ask you this favor," he replied, folding his arms across his chest in frustration.

"A favor is a hard ask when you have cost me so much time with my husband." She slouched back away from the man and glanced out the window. She thought for a moment that she could see Logan looking back at her from the glass, and she knew what her missing husband would want her to do. "And when it is done, you will take me to my husband?"

"I will personally make sure the two of you are in each other's arms again," he replied, looking at her.

"Where are we going?" Mia questioned.

She watched him sit back in his seat; a large smile graced the man's face, sending a chill down her back. "I have something to show you." He was having a tough time hiding his excitement now. A much different emotion took him over. "We will have to leave the train, though; your companions have already been sequestered."

"What do you mean sequestered?" Mia questioned.

"I cannot risk bringing any more on this journey. It is you alone," Hamilton stated as he stood with his hand out reached. "A crossroads as it were, take my hand and come with me, and I will show you sights you could have only dreamed of. And reunite you with my friend in the process."

There was no hesitation in her movement. It wasn't the hopes and dreams of an adventure that caused her to place her hand in his. She dreamed of seeing Logan's smile again. She started to grab her bag from the compartment above her, but he brushed past her and pulled it down. "I will carry your belongings," he said, and she followed him from the train car.

• • •

Mia could rarely remember seeing a building of its size. It engulfed the entire valley. Even in Boston, with all its glory, she could not remember seeing anything quite so large. There was not a dry stitch of clothing on her, and her horse stumbled on the harsh rocky ground. She was lighter than Hamilton. She could see the stress he was putting on his horse. "What is this place?" Mia sped up beside him.

"The future," he looked back, smiling. "Tomorrow, you and others will embark on a journey only imagined in fairy tales, Mrs. Ezekiel. Tomorrow is the future." Not even the darkness and rain could hide the excitement in the man's face.

He picked up the pace, and Mia kept her horse at his side. As they got closer, she could see the armed guards, at least a dozen, circling the perimeter of the building. She watched Hamilton dismount. She followed him out of the rain. She didn't realize how wet she was until they entered the building. The leather corset seemed much tighter, and the rest of her clothing clung to her with every movement. The guard on the inside of the door gave her a chill, so obviously observing her exposed cleavage.

"Come, come." The man moved fast for his size. She heard the doors lock behind her, and she rushed to keep up with the man. Down a long hall, she watched him unlock the door and hold it open for her. He moved much swifter than she expected for a man his size.

Mia understood his excitement when she entered the room. "I call it the Ulysses." Her mouth opened, and she was lost, completely uncertain as to what it was she was looking at. At first glance, it looked like a ship, but she knew there was no body of water nearby. The Ulysses towered over her, a large blimp-like oval as long as the building, and so tall that she wondered if she could even see the top. Attached below was a wooden structure that reminded her of the tavern back in Boston, though this was larger and three stories in height. Mia took a step back, feeling Hamilton's hand on her back. She hadn't even realized she had stepped in front of the man as she turned to look at him, looking at the vessel, a smile from ear to ear.

"Named for the president. Isn't she beautiful?" he said as he seemed to have to force himself to take his eyes off the vessel.

Mia looked from him back to the large unknown vessel, "What is it?"

"A ship, my dear Mrs. Ezekiel, and tomorrow, the Ulysses will lift from this site and cross the country. Faster than horse or train, we will soar across the sky," he again made himself look at her. She could see her own disbelief in what she was looking at in his unabashed pride and what he had a hand in creating.

"What do you mean?" she questioned, unsure of what she was hearing.

"The Ulysses is an airship!" his smile continued to fill his entire face as he blushed in the excitement of his words.

"But how?" Mia thought. Now, she was looking at a madman, and she glanced back at the ship and then at him. Her mouth was wide with questions about his sanity. Or her own. She couldn't quite comprehend what it was she was looking at.

"Come with me. I have someone else you need to meet," Hamilton turned, leading her down the hall as she looked back at the ship again. Mia hesitated, slowly leaving the room, not taking her eyes off the Ulysses. Not until she was out of the room, almost tripping over her own feet in the process.

Mia followed him into a room. "This is Sophia, my niece." The young girl had shoulder-length strawberry-blonde hair and a freckled face. Thin, but healthy for her age. She sat at a table with a journal in front of her. "And this is her other guardian, Kent Hardy. The two of you will share the responsibility of watching over her while you cross the country." The man sat in a corner, only pushing his cowboy hat up a moment to get a better look at her before pulling it back down over his eyes. She had spent little time in the western part of the states, but something about the man told her he was a hired gun, a gunslinger, and though she couldn't see his eyes, she could still feel them on her.

"Why does a little girl need two guardians… what aren't you telling me?" Mia questioned.

"Come, I'll show you to your room for the night. You can freshen up, and we can discuss this further," he replied.

• • •

"Sophia Hope is precious to me, Mia," Hamilton took a drink from his glass. "My sister, her mother, is currently in California. Sophia was staying with her father, but my brother-in-law has up and gone missing almost a year now, and Sophia has been in my care. I believe it is in the child's best interest as well as my own that she travels back to California where she can be with her mother." It dawned on her that the young girl's father and her husband had both been gone about the same amount of time, and it caused her to look back at the door wondering what the connection was, but now she bit down on her lip, locking it away until later.

"You're still not telling me the reasons she needs two guardians," Mia forcefully questioned.

"My dear sister believes her absent husband is more than missing but dead." Hamilton investigated the fire. He was still in the wet clothes from the ride in. "My brother-in-law had many enemies; he agitated many wealthy people in the South during the wars, and he was a lawyer and observer of sorts, much like your Logan. He acquired many stories from freed slaves since the war about their former owners and their practices. Stories people would like to see kept quiet, I believe. His heart was his downfall."

Mia took a drink of her own. "And you believe someone would go as far to harm the little girl to get back at the father?"

"It's delicate times, Mia," Hamilton replied. "You should get some sleep. You are in for a long day tomorrow."

Mia smiled as she bowed so slightly, her clothing still wet as she turned and left the room. She passed by the room where Hardy and Sophia were and kept going, recalling her steps from where she last saw the Ulysses. As she approached the door, the same man who had made her feel uncomfortable stepped into her path.

"Can I help you, ma'am?" he questioned.

"What is your name?" It wasn't what she wanted to ask, but it fell forward.

"Rory Campbell, ma'am," he answered. "Can I help you?"

"No," she replied. She started to step around him, but he stepped into her path.

"No one is permitted in the hangar without an escort, ma'am," he stated as he smirked. She hadn't realized it before; she was taller than the man, and his eyes seemed to focus on her exposed neck, causing her to place a hand over the collar she all but forgot she was wearing, the cold derringer still there hidden from sight. "Even wearing that," he said with a nod. It was a Brotherhood pendant, just a small symbol of a small feather floating above a flame, no description beyond those etchings. When Logan had given it to her, she didn't even notice what the symbol truly was. Logan designed it shortly after they were married. Besides her and Logan, she only knew of a few select people who would recognize it.

"I'm sorry," she took a step back away from the man, and he took a step forward toward her.

"I can escort you back to your room," he replied. He grinned eerily at the prospect of escorting her, and it sent a chill down her back as she lowered her hand to the top of the dress, one finger slipping into her cleavage across the top of the small pistol.

"That won't be necessary," she said, taking a long, deep breath and turning. With a few quick steps, she moved away from the man. She couldn't help but look over her shoulder, and he was still there watching her as she fled.

Mia reached the edge of the wilderness and turned back, looking at the structure, and it still caused her alarm at its size. The rain was slowing to no more than a sprinkle now. And she stood straight, feeling the cool wind graze across her skin. It was so gentle that it reminded her of the last morning she'd spent with Logan before his departure. *Kiss me again before you go.* She remembered her last words to him, and it fell on her as if the world was caving in on herself. Her tears began to fall with ease. No matter what Hamilton Bastion said, Logan wasn't alive.

Chapter Two

"Logan is dead," the voice growled at her.

Mia didn't sleep, or if she had, it was only for a few moments, as the exhaustion of the past few days placed a near-unbearable weight on her. She kept wanting to sneak back in and look at the Ulysses, but after her first attempt, she couldn't bring herself to have another confrontation so soon. She knew it was likely she would pull the small pistol on the next occasion she had a run-in with Rory Campbell. She didn't even feel comfortable staying in the room she had been given. She found herself sitting outside the building at the edge of the timberline, watching the wagon after a wagon of people and supplies arrived. Dozens upon dozens of men. Even at the distance, she felt out of place. Most of the new arrivals were men, white men. This made her feel uncomfortable. Mia's hair was as black as the feathers of a crow, set in a faux hawk. A few loose strands of hair floated wildly around the back of her neck. Her hands were bound in fingerless black leather gloves, and the rest of her arms were bare to her shoulders, except for a tight fishnet stocking going from her gloves all the way up to her elbows. Two leather necklaces hung around her neck, creased with age and wear, one with a small white feather secured to the end, tickling her skin. After the confrontation with Campbell, she put the pendant her husband had made for her away for safekeeping. A black corset and bustle over her white blouse, at times, caused an awkward pain when she took a deep breath. A loose black pinstriped vest with hand-sewn straps held her weapon of choice, a small axe. It had been years since she had used it for its true nature, violence. Maybe it was the security of the weapon her father had taught her how to use; it reminded her of him, and she needed comfort now more than ever. She felt the small single-shell pistol in her garter, a weapon much harder to retrieve. The cool touch of steel on her thigh often sent a chill up her back when she least expected it, but she thought it safer there than in her bustle, where she knew it would likely make an appearance as soon as she had another uncomfortable confrontation. She had two Colt pistols squared away in her bags, but the last thing she wanted to do was to wear them openly.

"You must be Mia Ezekiel."

Mia shifted to look at a large man, over six feet tall and looking like a mountain, sitting on top of his black and white horse who had managed to not only slip up on her but was also close enough if he were to dismount, she would be within arm's reach of the large man. It amazed her. He was so substantial in size that he made her recollection of Benson seem small. "Who is asking?"

The man smirked as he repositioned himself in his saddle and looked off toward the complex. His new position made him look even larger. He seemed to block out any light the waning moon was casting. He looked fresh, his long dark hair was wet, and his skin seemed to glow. He had just come from a bath somewhere in the wilderness. The thought of it sent a chill over her entire body; it was nearly freezing outside, but he still took the time for a proper bath. He looked like no man she had ever seen before, and she felt his presence. There was something about him that caused a sense of both excitement and fear. "Hamilton said you had spirit; I don't believe he realizes how much."

"Don't pretend to know me," Mia quickly replied, taking a couple steps back from the shadow he cast. Her left hand lowered, and she could have easily pulled the small axe, but even she wasn't sure she could do so before he was upon her if he wanted.

The large man laughed, leaning forward on his horse. "I do know you."

Mia gritted her teeth. He was arrogant, and his confident-filled swagger set her off unexpectedly.

"But I fear I am being ungentlemanly," he smirked. "My name is Gareth, and Hamilton told me you left the complex this morning and wanted me to retrieve you. It is nearly time."

Mia turned back to get a look at the complex. It made her feel uneasy knowing she had been noticed leaving the complex by someone when she had tried to slip away. "Do you know what is in there?"

"Yes," Gareth replied. She heard the man dismount. "Rather ingenious when you consider what the mind is capable of. But I digress. I'm hired muscle. No one truly asks or cares about my insights." She turned. He was smiling. She was surprised at how well he knew what he was. Hired muscle, and he fit the build. His shirt was unbuttoned, his arms exposed in the long white sleeve shirt. He was an exceptionally large man. She also realized that it was all likely a ruse, a well, muscular disguised ruse to hide what the man was truly capable of, and the way he spoke was enough to make her realize he was more than he seemed.

"Hired muscle," she smirked, realizing there wasn't much difference between the two of them. And she knew what he meant, the untamed look in his eyes. They were alike, which told her more about the man. He could not be trusted. "So why are you going on this…" Mia hesitated, "Journey?"

"Money, why else?" Gareth's voice was deep and raspy, and he ended each sentence with a hint of laughter. Mia knew instantly it was a lie. "Hamilton has promised a very hefty purse awaits me on the other coast."

"There are more important things in this world than money," Mia said, going along with it.

"Like love?" There was the hint of laughter again, and it angered Mia more than the fact that she knew he was lying to her.

"A lifetime ago, I would have agreed," the man now stood beside her, towering over her. The hint of laughter was gone in the one sentence.

Mia lowered, running her hands through the dirt and watching it fall through her exposed fingers. "So many soldiers."

"The stench of young, impressionable men pollutes the air." The laugh was back. "One could almost say they were naive. When you were their age… did you understand the world or even who you were?"

Mia laughed. Gareth reminded her of someone, a scout she once knew a long time ago. "We need to go," he stated, pulling the horse along in front of her. She followed suit.

Mia entered the main hangar of the building. Gareth was only steps behind her. There were at least twenty-five people gathered in the hangar. And most of their eyes were on her. She snarled. The closest man to her took an immediate step back, and she could read his lips as he mouthed a slur in her direction.

"I will not bless this," a loud voice called out. It broke the gazes on her. She saw the man with his arms raised high, Bible in hand. "This… this unholy abomination," she could see the disappointed look on Hamilton's face. Mia could see the others around them, and people began to move away from them. But more obvious, moving away from the airship. Like the air was suctioned out of the room, people became pail.

The crowd parted, and at least half of the gathering followed the preacher from the Ulysses. Mia watched Hamilton closely. His demeanor did not change. "What are you going to do now, Mr. Bastion?" a young man questioned.

"The Ulysses will lift off as planned." Hamilton smiled as he counted how many people remained. He turned to place a whistle to his lips, and he let loose two long-winded screeches. It was only a moment before the sound of the airship's engine started. It roared through the hangar. It was louder than two trains side by side, and the ship lifted off the ground.

Mia's heart raced, realizing he truly wasn't crazed... She backed away until she could go no further, a dull thud as she hit Gareth in the chest. She looked back at him, and he only smiled. But he wasn't looking at her, like everyone else but her. He was looking at Ulysses. "Brilliant," she saw his lips move, only because she was so close. She could hear his muttering and almost taste his breathing as he breathed. Berries. His breath smelled of fresh berries.

"This is crazy," Mia turned back, looking at the Ulysses.

"I want to go," she heard the young man closest to Hamilton say out loud. She couldn't see his face but could hear the wonderment in his voice. Everyone was amazed. She half expected those who had retreated to return as she turned to look at the door, but only one figure stood at the entrance to the hangar. The preacher, and even from the distance between them, she could see his disgruntled features.

"I'm afraid there will be no journalists on this voyage," Hamilton said.

"This is history. It should be recorded," the young man replied.

"Mrs. Ezekiel," Mia broke from her gaze on the Ulysses to look at Hamilton. "You need to retrieve your bags and my niece. The Ulysses will deport…" He looked down at his watch, and his smile grew, "ten minutes and counting. Right on time."

Mia stepped away from Gareth and watched as the large man stepped up close to Hamilton, and the inventor whispered something into the taller man's ear, and then the mastermind behind the airship was gone from sight.

Mia entered her room, surprised to see Sophia sitting on the bed with three bags beside her. "Where is Mr. Hardy?" she questioned. The sound of a gun having the hammer closed broke her gaze. She turned, watching the man holster his weapon.

Mia tilted her head to one side, looking at him. He crossed the room, grabbed all their bags, and turned. He approached without a word. She hesitated and realized he was waiting for her to open the door. As he rushed past, she felt the tug of the young girl's hand on her own. She did not know what to say as she followed the Marshal. Why did he have his gun out?

As they reached the Ulysses, all the men that were there before were now gone. Those who were there were in a rush, herself and her companions included. Hardy never broke stride, and Sophia tugged her along. As they walked up the ramp into the Ulysses, she saw a soldier there waiting. "The last of our passengers," the young man smiled, taking the bags from Hardy. She had expected it to be Rory Campbell, but she had not seen this young man before. "I will put these in your respective rooms." She observed the young man; his pistols, though holstered, were not latched safely into their place. It was obvious he had been ordered to use them on anyone who dared to try to come aboard who was not welcomed.

As she passed the threshold, Mia felt the young girl's grip tighten. The doors of the Ulysses sealing behind them made a loud screech as gears locked the bolts tightly around the door. There was no escape now. No turning back. Air compressing, fleeing out through vents, whistled, sending a cold chill up Mia's back. The temperature in the hanger rose immediately, causing her to take a deep breath, and sweat began to bead on her forehead. "It's all right." She looked down into Sophia's pale green eyes. She was unsure if she was trying to convince her ward or herself.

Chapter Three

The young soldier would take three steps and look back. His facial expression never once changed from a sneer of disapproval. Three more steps and looking back, it was an easy pattern for Mia to notice, and each time the young man glanced back, his left hand seemed to be a little closer to the unsecured pistol on the man's hip. He would rarely look at Sophia or Hardy. All the time, he glared at her. He went up two staircases until he held the door open for them, leading out into a mess hall. His glare made her feel uneasy each time their eyes met, but she tried not to let it show. There was a lot to take in, the decor of the ship and the craftsmanship, but the man was such a distraction on their walk that he was the only thing she watched.

Mia attempted to replicate his sneer back at him, and when they stepped through the door, there was an almost shocked look mixed in with his look of disdain. This may not have been the same soldier from the day before, but he held the same menacing glare.

"Meals will be served three times daily, 0700, 1200, and 1700 hours. There will be a bell chimed when it is served. It is up to you to make yourself present for the courses." He watched closely as they all passed. "I am Frost," he stated, closing the door behind him. "For the entirety of the journey to California, the three of you are prohibited to leave this level or the observation deck." She watched as the man secured the door they had just entered, careful to lock it behind him and place the master key to the lock inside his pressed uniform.

"Observation deck?" Mia questioned, looking around the mess hall to a corridor leading to a long hallway with many doors on each side.

The soldier brushed past her, leading them down the hallway that looked oddly like a train corridor she had been riding in days before; the walls were dark mahogany in color with brace railing about waist high on both sides of the wall. The lights above each door were bottled lamp lights not too dissimilar to the ones she remembered from the streets of Boston, complete with glitches every so often, making it seem haunted. "You are lucky. The Ulysses was built to house up to twenty guests. But there are just the three of you and plenty of rooms to choose from. Each room has a key that is all its own, and you will need to always keep it on your person. The captain is the only individual with a skeleton key who can open all doors aboard the ship. You will respect your other passenger's privacy; you will follow the rules as put forth to you, and you will not make things difficult in any manner." Over half of the lights in the hallways seemed to glitch at once, and Sophia stopped moving from her position in front of the group. Mia placed a hand on the young girl's shoulder, getting a worried look back. "It's okay," she smiled to reassure the girl before turning her attention back to Frost, who was glaring at her. "Who is the captain?" Mia questioned.

"You will meet him in due time," Frost sneered at her as he stopped in the middle of the hall. "You may choose your rooms." Mia watched Hardy walk over, opening a door on the right-hand side of the hall. Frost replied as he plucked a key from the ring for his room and handed it over. Hardy did not step inside the room. He set his bags down in the hallways and then turned in the doorway, his eyes still mostly hidden, but she could see him as he watched Sofia.

Mia knelt, looking at Sofia. "You can choose our room if you want." Mia looked up at Hardy and then Frost.

The girl gave a shy smile before brushing past Frost down the hall, two doors on the left, the room directly across from Hardy. She observed as the young girl looked to Hardy before Frost over even herself. "Her choice." Frost handed Mia the key, but he was a touch shorter than her. She imagined it was an issue for him as he glared up into her eyes, in part because her boots gave her the height advantage. She found it odd how easily men were bothered when a woman was taller than them. It was a fact Mia had gotten used to quelling since youth. Both Rory Campbell and Frost were shorter in stature than her, but she was also certain her height wasn't the only reason they held such disdain for her. She had managed to keep clear of Campbell, but she figured in such a small, confined space aboard the Ulysses, she wouldn't be able to avoid Frost so easily.

"Stand up straight," she heard the voice order her, much like her mother used to do when she would slouch.

"You mentioned an observation deck?" Mia questioned again. She could see the man grit his teeth. Mia looked down at him, even standing a touch straighter on the front of her feet, and she couldn't stop herself from smiling. She could see the blood rush from his face as his eyes narrowed.

"The stairway at the end of the hall leads to the observation deck. I would suggest you be careful. It is still an incredibly open design," Frost sneered again, brushing past her. Mia watched until the man was gone.

"I will take first watch over Sofia if you want," Hardy said. The gunslinger was looking at the little girl and not at

Mia. She wondered as she had before why a little girl needed round-the-clock protection, but she noticed the girl had a preference for the hired gun, and the gritty-looking man seemed to also prefer the little girl be at his side. Mia smiled as she looked at the girl who didn't so much as look for approval before she rushed to the man's room and shut the door behind them. Mia reached down, picking up her bag. As she walked to her room, she put it just inside the door before closing it, quickly making sure it was locked. She didn't entirely trust Frost, and what he said was just as likely the young soldier also had a key to all the rooms all his own.

The room was dark once the door was shut. She had hoped the heat from the rest of the Ulysses would be different in the room, but it was sweltering, even in the confined room. She placed her bag in the nearest corner before falling back onto the bed. There was so limited light inside the room, considering it was daylight on the outside, but she had not slept the night before, and despite the heat, it was only a few minutes after she had laid down she fell fast asleep.

• • •

Mia was unsure of how much time had passed when she woke, but she knew she needed air. She quickly left her room, turned left, and slowly went up the stairs. She came to a door, and as she stepped through, the cool air caused her to take a deep breath. She closed her eyes, stepping outward. The sound of the door closing caused her to open her eyes. Her smile grew. It wasn't the large deck or the hum of the engines of the Ulysses, or even the large blimp canvas overhead. It was the sky beyond it all that made her smile. She strolled toward the outer railing, her steps getting slower and closer to one another as she approached. She was close enough to see more than the sky now. The winter mountains in the distance, snow top peaks, and the dull colors in the valleys. She couldn't fight back the smile. The view had taken her breath away. Mia leaned over the railing, the sun on her face. Brittle chilly air bit her exposed golden skin, causing goose pimples to rise. She had not even noticed the cold till now. Her raspberry lips formed an unforced smile. She wanted so badly to leave the ghosts of her past locked away in the back of her mind and focus on her situation. The first moment she saw Ulysses, she thought of nothing but the magnificent vessel, but now, she found herself thinking about him again. Wishing he were here at her side to see such a marvelous view. "Logan," she lowered her head, closing her eyes. "I wish you were here to see this. Oh, how I wish you were here to see this, my love."

The sound of the propellers and howling wind was deafening and masked the approach of another. "Should not be alone out here," he hissed as he slithered to the railing, a safe distance from her.

Mia looked at the thin man, almost frail in his army blues, as they blew freely in the wind. "Who are you?" Mia growled.

"You know me," the man stated. She couldn't see his face, but her reflection looked back at her, shining in the dull bronze mask. "I'm the captain of this ship."   Mia felt his eyes upon her; hatred and anguish filled his blue eyes, and his voice had a familiar tenge as he spoke. "My brother's greatest accomplishment."

"Not him!" The voice grumbled.

Mia gasped. Why hadn't Hamilton told her he would be the Captain of the Ulysses? She knew why he wore the mask. The two of them shared history, and she imagined all the reasons Hamilton had kept this piece of information from her. She would have backed out.

Julian Bastion was thin, frail in his freshly pressed army blues. He was taller than her but no more than six feet in height, made to seem bigger by his thick, polished boots. A reinforced masquerade mask held to his face by two-inch-wide leather straps. His eyes, a pale distant blue, always reflected the bronze from the interior of the mask. A scar crossed his forehead down from his thinning light brown hair until it was lost from sight by the mask. Mia dug her fingernails into her palm. It had been ages since she had seen the man.

"Fancy words, fancy clothes, and a fancy name do not change what you were born," he hissed in a low, gravelly voice. He stood still a distance from her. Julian was a fighter when she first met him, and now, he seemed a frail impersonator from a phantom play as he stood almost ready for her to strike him down with little fight. She thought she could even see his hand tremble with fear.

Mia's face reddened; she could feel the blush of anger against the frigid air. Her angry sneer turned to a wicked smile as she spoke, "I am here because your brother saw me as a worthy guardian for your niece. Does not say much about how he feels about your hate for the woman… who nearly killed you so many years ago, does it?"

"If not for Logan Ezekiel, you would have been hung till your pretty little neck snapped, with your throat slit by my blade," he said. She could tell his jaw twisted as he gritted his teeth.

"Never was one for a fair fight, were you, Julian." Mia took a quick step forward. The man recoiled, taking several steps back and using the railing to hold him up, but she saw the grip he had on the bar. He was much stronger than his appearance showed; he was putting on an act and attempting to bait her into a fight. "You will not mention my husband's name to me again this trip, Mr. Bastion." Her hand twitched, digging her nails deeper into her palm. She ached to go for the sharp axe hidden inside the vest. It would only take a moment to overpower the man, split his skull, and push him over the edge. She had done it twice over in her mind as she watched him pretend to cower. It was that pretense that caused her alarm.

Julian raised his hands at his side. "It is the last I will mention the fool of a good man." He walked away while keeping a careful watch until he was gone. She turned to let the breeze calm her anger. It had been over a year since she heard her late husband's voice. In her heart, she knew he was dead. There was nothing that could have kept him away, not even something as magical as Ulysses, or so she'd hoped.

• • •

The bell rang. It was the dinner bell, only made more obvious by the growing darkness. Mia gave a last fleeting glance out into the distance of the Ulysses. Opening the door, the heat from the interior of the vessel took her breath away.

She stood there for a moment, wondering if she was truly as hungry as she'd thought. She shut the door behind her as she quickly descended the dark stairwell to the next level of the ship. Hurrying past several doors, stopping only when she reached Hardy's. She gave a quick knock, waiting for a reply. Hardy opened the door, his hand resting on the handle of his revolver. The man was more prepared than her to watch over the young girl, so maybe it was a good thing that they preferred each other's company.

Mia stepped inside and surveyed the room, and then she saw the young girl. Sitting in a corner with a book in hand, only looking up when Mia cleared her throat. The girl's eyes made even the hardest of a ruffian smile. Shoulder-length curly auburn locks, in the dim light of the cabin, almost dirt brown, but the day Mia met the girl, they looked as red as a rose petal. Light freckles littered the young girl's face. She smiled when Mia smiled, and her cheeks a bright red of innocent youth. She wore a simple flowered dress; her petite fingers held the book close as she stood on her bare feet. Though the girl had not said so, Mia knew immediately she hated wearing shoes by how much she had fidgeted in them when they first met.

"Supper is ready," Mia said, holding out her hand, and the little girl placed her tiny hand in her grasp. She led her down the hall to the mess station, where a long oak table with matching chairs waited. It was suitable for dining twenty and took up most of the room.

"Mia Ezekiel." Gareth's hearty smile seemed to light up the room when she walked in. It took her by surprise. She even fought against smiling when she saw him, though she wouldn't be able to explain why. He was one of two men sitting at the massive table. Both were already eating. "Welcome," he said.

Mia nodded, helping the little girl up into her seat, Mia hadn't had much experience with children, but she was sure at Sophia's age and size, she didn't exactly need a lot of help, let alone getting up into a chair. "Gareth." She found herself continuing to smile and had to look away to make herself stop. She could see it in his dark eyes, he had noticed, and it made an uneasy feeling in her stomach. He was much more intelligent than he played at being, but she was beginning to realize there were a lot of people on the ship pretending to be something they weren't. Her thoughts rested on how frail Julian had acted when they confronted each other on the observation deck.

"This, ladies, is my companion in the pit of hell…" The man looked at Sophia, and his regret took over for his language. "Sorry, the boiler of the Ulysses, where I work with your friend Gareth."

She watched the other man for a second. He seemed to stare right directly through her; his cheeks were red, and his skin flushed from exhaustion. "I don't believe we've met," Mia said, lowering herself across the table in an attempt to shake the man's hand.

"I'm sorry, miss, you don't want to shake my filthy hands," he said, a drink dribbling out of the side of his mouth down his beard. "I'm Rodney Stone." Mia smiled a little less watching the man. She had to force herself to look at the other.

The man held his cup high, greeting them. He looked mostly at Sophia now, making Mia give him a questioning glare. "Your daughter, what is her name?" She stood behind Sophia's chair with an arm placed on the top and watched him. Stone was a bigger man, but she could mostly only tell about his weight from her position across from him at the table.

"Sophia," Mia replied, knowing there was no resemblance between the two of them.

"She reminds me of my own. Sorry for my lingering glare, it's the"   he made a motion across his face—"the freckles. It's such an adorable trait on a girl, I had them when I was a lad, and they were the joke of all the other kids around me. So distinct." She watched as the man stood and walked to the back table to refill his cup.

She looked at Gareth and thought that the two men could not be any more different in appearance. Rodney Stone was a short man, five foot four on his best day and nearly three hundred pounds in weight. His shoulder-length hair was twisted and matted; his beard reached his chest, which was the same in distress, both filled with grayer than the former black of his youth. In his mid to late forties, his skin was white and wrinkled beyond his years, hiding any trace of a freckle. Stone returned to the table, and before he sat, he wrinkled his face up, looking odd, and her ward instantly laughed. He smiled when he got his intended reaction, which made her feel at ease with the man. Mia had a vastly different reaction to him and his attention to the girl; she was uncomfortable, and she had found herself still standing at the back of the chair, fidgeting.

Gareth smiled, but he was not looking at Sophia; he was looking at Mia. "You both work in the engine room?" Mia questioned, trying to take her mind off her uncomfortable feelings.

Stone let out a chuckle and looked at Gareth. She could not imagine the wonders it took to keep the ship afloat so high in the sky. She could smell them from the opposite end of the table. Sweat, wood, coal, and steam, she could see it clinging to their skin. The two men raised their cups and smiled at her, wasting little time as they returned to the food in front of them, and by the crumbs around their plates, they were at least on their second serving. It was a rule on the Ulysses—first come, first serve when the bell sounded.

Even while he ate, Gareth watched her, and she found it frustrating and hard to gauge the man with his eyes always on her. With his shoulder-length dark wavy hair, dark skin that was always clean-shaven, and in his mid to late thirties, the man was in peak physical shape. Even now, his shirt was unbuttoned and free to move when the low circulating breeze of the Ulysses did so. His expressions gave speeches about what was on his mind. It was a smile she often tried not to respond to, but even she could not deny the man was hard not to stare at, and for a moment, she thought about their meeting in the woods and his berry-scented breath. She knew from then he cleaned up nicely, and though he was sitting now, she could easily remember his size as she had to stand looking up into the man's eyes.

Mia made sure Sophia was secure in her seat, completely on the other side of the table from the two men and the food, before she retrieved a silver bowl and plate from a small cart. The evening meal looked like a soup of vegetables and potatoes, and what she hoped for was a roasted pig. She picked through it all until she was happy with the serving size for her ward. She returned and sat them in front of Sophia as she gave only a small glance at the food. Mia watched as she scooted to the table, lowered her head to say a small prayer, and began to pick at the soup with her spoon. She smiled when she watched her take her first bite. She then turned to getting her own.

Mia had just spooned the soup into her bowl when Bastion stepped into the room. He glared at her before walking to the opposite end of the table from where she would be sitting. He did stop to mess with Sophia's hair for a moment and shared a redeeming smile between the two of them. He stepped up to his chair, removed his thick blue jacket, and laid it across the back of the highchair neatly so it would not crease. It was hard to imagine how uncomfortable he was in the thick wool jacket inside the sweltering vessel. He undid the buttons on the sleeves of his shirt and carefully rolled them up to his arms in perfection; it was his way of allowing her to get back to her seat before he started to gather food. She was sure and almost thankful for his actions.

Julian had just finished gathering his own and taken his seat when a man entered from the door opposite the one she had entered. The Black man had a book in hand and sat on the table opposite Mia. "I have been told your ward likes to read. Maybe she might like this." Mia started to reach for it, but Sophia quickly grabbed it, pulling it close to her side.

"This is William Beck." Mia looked at Gareth upon hearing his voice.

William Beck's head was clean-shaven, and he had a thick black beard. He was in his early to mid-thirties, and he was smiling. He gathered his food quickly and took a seat nearest Julian. He only gave her a nod as he sat, Mia replied with one of her own. She looked to Sophia to see the young girl already looking through the worn book.

Kent Hardy entered the room behind her back. He gave an intense glare that would send a chill down anyone's back and cause the hairs on one's arms to stand straight. His eyes were deep brown, and he was white but tanned from too much time in the sun and on horseback. Short, straight brown hair and a hint of a beard he had shaved the day before the vessel set to the sky. Kent only took a bowl of soup, found a seat evenly spaced away from everyone else, and calmly began eating.

Mia sat watching each man at the table, a glance back and forth between each of them. One of these men was likely there to kill the little girl at her side. It was painful to even consider not one of them did much except look at the food in front of them, and her heart raced when she realized how little she knew about them. Except for Julian Bastion, she knew more than she wanted and hated the man, but would he kill his niece? Doubtful. At least she was sure she could trust that much about the man. The unknown scared her. She allowed a hand to disappear under the table and run across her right upper leg. The small pistol was there, and even though she could hardly feel it for the clothing, she could still feel the cool touch against her skin. The axe still pressed and pinched against her breast. She did not have to reach for it. It was just like her hand—it was always there.

Her eyes settled on Kent Hardy, the only other man on the Ulysses permitted to have anything other than a blade. Hamilton Bastion handpicked everyone, down to the cook who would make the maiden journey. Why would he be willing to permit one to make the journey if he knew they wished harm to the child? Mia glanced down to her left. Curls hid a lot of the little girl's face, but she looked up at her with a smile. Mia returned it before she again looked at the men at the table and the sounds of them chewing their food.

Kent Hardy may have been the last to sit at the table, but he was the first to finish his meal, the bowl still half full before he stood and left the room. Mia watched every step the man took until he was nearly out of the room before he glanced at Sophia, confirming the connection between the young girl and the man, though Mia couldn't quite figure out why. This wasn't just a job for Kent Hardy; he cared deeply for the girl.

Rodney and Gareth still shoveled food like it was their last meal and paid little attention to anything else. William Beck looked from the food in front of him as he messed with the soup with his spoon to the book opened in his other hand. Julian Bastion cut every piece of meat to a bite size small enough for a mouse before placing it in his mouth, taking exceptional care to never touch anything without a utensil. One thing Mia was sure of was she could not just sit by and wait for one of them to make an attempt on the little girl's life; she had to know more about them.

It was then the little girl placed a hand on her arm, startled her from her concentration. She looked at her, a big smile with the food pushed away. She had eaten even more than Mia, and she nodded as she stood. The walk back to the cabin was a brisk one, and the little girl had no problem keeping pace with the longer-legged woman. She seemed to skip at her own pace, and at times, was ahead of her guardian.

Back inside Sophia's room, Mia took a seat on the bed while the young girl again sat on the floor, opening her book back to the saved page. The girl looked at the door, and she didn't have to guess what the child wanted. She wanted to spend time with her, but as her head fell back to the pillow, she felt the exhaustion take hold.

Chapter Four

Mia was jolted from her sleep, leaping out of the bed. She was still in her constricted clothing from the night before. She was covered in sweat, and the walls seemed to close in around her. She glanced over at Sophia; she'd been asleep as well. Under covers, Mia did not know how the young girl looked so comfortable and cool. Mia was flushed. She needed cool water, a breeze, a fresh breath of uncirculated air, and just about anything else that would have helped her in the current situation.

The siren echoed throughout the room. Maybe it was part of the reason she had woken up. The siren would blare horrifyingly loud for one moment and then stop. Mia gasped when someone pounded on the door. She knew it was going to be Kent, but she still could not risk it. She pulled the derringer from its spot on her guard and approached the door. Just as she touched the handle, the siren blared again. Mia glared back at Sophia, who hadn't so much as moved a hair.

She let it creep open to see Kent. He looked down the hall. He was ghostly white and obviously worried about Sophia. "Is Sophia…?"

Mia could see the terror on his face as she looked back in the direction of the little girl, who now sat up with her eyes wide. "She is awake," Mia let the door open so he could see her. "If you don't mind…"

"You look like you're running a fever," he stated when he looked at her again.

"It's the air in here. It circulates but only seems to get hotter with each passing second," she stated. She pulled at her dress, placing the gun back in its place on the inner thigh. She blushed with embarrassment, not realizing she had done it. When she looked up, having secured the weapon, she met the man's eyes.

"Get you a breath of air. I'll watch over Sofia for a few hours." Kent walked past her into the room without waiting for a reply. Mia didn't hesitate as she grabbed the key to her room from the table nearest the door and headed out.

Mia let the door shut behind her. She looked down the hall, waiting for the siren to sound again, but it must have finally stopped. She wondered, as badly as she needed a breath. She wanted to know what the cause of the commotion was. Was Ulysses about to plummet to the ground below? She would at least like to know beforehand.

She went away from the stairway, passing by the table and to the stairway leading downward. She could hear voices but could not make out what they were saying. She slowly crept down the staircase. There was no hesitation, though she could remember Frost telling her she and the others were to stay on the guest level. The voices got louder as she got closer to the next level until she heard the first clear words. "Who are you?" It was Julian's voice asking the question. Knowing he was there did not stop her progression. It only made her more curious about what the captain would be up to at this hour.

Mia entered the hallway. Julian stood over a man sitting at the table. She recognized the young man, even at their distance. It was the reporter who was trying to convince Hamilton to let him go on the trip.

"You're not supposed to be here." Frost saw her. He was standing at the young man's side.

Julian looked at her; he was wearing his mask, but she could feel the man's eyes on her.

"My name is Christian Owen. I'm a reporter…."

"I saw him with Hamilton," Mia spoke louder as she approached. She glared at Frost. "I wanted to know what the

siren was for and if we were all about to die when this…
thing… crashes to the earth."

The young man couldn't have been much over twenty,
his eyes a dark blue. She could see the start of a beard from
her position in the dim light. "Why did you stow away?"

"Are you kidding?" The kid's face was filled with
excitement. Was he a threat to Sophia or just an eager kid
who didn't want to take no for an answer? "This… this
vessel, it's amazing. This journey… it should be recorded…"

Mia could hear Julian laugh. "And if I was to confine
you to quarters for the entirety of this journey? What will you
have then?"

"I will still have the story," Owen couldn't stop
smiling. She could see the anger in Frost's face. It wasn't at
the young man. He kept glaring at her. It was only a moment
before Frost broke from his side coming toward her.

"I told you, you are not allowed off the guest level."
The man grabbed her arm forcefully and attempted to walk
past, dragging her along. She thought she heard a snicker
coming from Julian's direction, as if he knew what was going
to happen. She grabbed the man's wrist, twisted, and pushed
until he was forced into the wall.

"Do not touch me again," Mia growled so close to his ear for a moment that she thought about latching onto the soft flesh and ripping it away.

"Act like civilized people, the both of you," Julian said. But Mia knew he was mostly referring to her. She let her grip loosen and stepped back away. Frost straightened his uniform as he turned, looking at her, then at the captain. "Escort young Mr. Owen to a room," Julian began to straighten his uniform, putting his jacket back on.

Mia started up the stairs, but she was not going to wait until Frost caught her with the young man. She could even hear them starting up the stairs behind her as she reached the top. She did not stop until she was safely inside her room. Sophia was asleep in her bed, and Hardy was curled up on the floor asleep. She took a deep breath; she wasn't as hot as she was before she woke. She slowly walked to the bed, reaching behind to loosen the corset. The moment it was free, it felt better. She could breathe easier. She set it beside the bed and rolled over onto her back. She pulled the sheet up partially onto her and fell quickly to sleep.

· · ·

Mia woke, rolling over to look for Sophia, noticing immediately the girl was gone, as was Hardy. She knew wherever the girl was, she was safe with the other guardian.

She stood from the bed, grabbing the overcoat, showing no worry for the corset as she pulled it over her. She barely remembered removing half of her clothing when she came back to the room. She strolled out into the hallway and gave three soft knocks on his door with no answer. Mia gritted her teeth with frustration as she approached the observation deck. She was hot but not as feverish as before.

Immediately upon stepping out the door, Mia breathed in the cool, brisk air. It was still dark, but lamps illuminated the deck. She could feel the snow on the breeze before she opened her eyes. She did not expect to see Kent Hardy sitting with his long-rimmed cowboy hat pulled down over his eyes.

Hearing Sophia sitting near the door grabbed her attention immediately. The girl smiled as she looked up from her book. "Are you cold, little one?"

Sophia shook her head no.

Mia approached Hardy. He was motionless with his back to the railing. She approached, holding her arms across her body, fighting against the unexpected chill. It was something that never bothered her before, but now she found, at times, she preferred the touch of the flame to the chill of the frost. "I did not expect anyone to be up here," Mia claimed as she stood with her back against the rail. Strands of hair fell across her face long past being anything but a mess that she would attend to later.

Kent lifted his hat, and she immediately noticed his eyes, and it made sense now why the man said so little. Why he ate so little, and why was he now sitting near the rail of the viewing deck. She could see his stomach and chest heave forcefully.

"I am sure Frost has something to help with the sickness," Mia stated, turning to lean forward and face the cool sky air.

"I will be fine…. we land for our first stop in two days. The touch of the ground will ease my sickness, ma'am," Kent said, placing the hat at his side, leaning his head back against the rail, and taking a deep breath. Mia noticed his eyes were on Sophia; he was a much better guardian than she was. The young girl seemed to go to him on instinct.

"Ma'am, it was strange to hear, and she was unsure how it made her feel even after all these years. Part of her hated it almost as much as being called a 'squaw' even though the tone Kent used it in was out of respect. "I don't mean to be forward, Mr. Hardy," Mia turned only slightly to look down at the man. "The girl has taken to you. Why was I needed when you could have likely handled the job as easily as the two of us?"

"I have ties to the Hope family, which is why the girl takes to me with such ease. I've known her since her birth; her father was like a brother to me growing up. I told Sir Bastion I could care for her and that I needed no help. I even questioned Sir Bastion's choice," Kent stated. "Yes, I am all too familiar with your… past. This is not the life expected of you. Your parents come from two vastly different lives, and then there is Logan…"

"You know an awful lot about me, and I know very little about you or anyone else on this vessel…"

Kent Hardy smiled. It was the only time she had seen the man give any noticeable expression. Silent eyes looked up to her, and as he moved his hand, her heart skipped a beat. He pulled the vest to one side past the holstered gun, and a badge shone in the dim light. "In fairness, you are right; you do deserve to know… I am a Marshal, but I am guessing that means truly little to you. Did anyone tell you how it was young Sophia who came to the station the day the Ulysses took off? Why is her father missing, and her mother is in California?"

Mia frowned and realized the man knew more about Sophia than she did. "My father and Sophia's father's father were brothers, Ms. Ezekiel. I brought her down to Washington so she could make this trip across the country to be with her mother. When I was briefed, I laughed at the idea of… this ship. Then, the day it took off before my very eyes, the propellers, the large puffs of steam… I thought it was a dream. I saw your face too, darling, the same wide-eyed look of crazy I know I had." Kent Hardy hid the badge away as he used the railing to pull his weight from the floor and into a standing position.

"Do you believe Sophia's life is in danger?" Mia questioned. Both looked back at the young girl lost in her book.

"Unfortunately, I do," Kent replied.

"Why, what kind of monster would hurt a little girl?" Mia grumbled.

"Better question. Why would she need so much protection if every man on this journey was handpicked by Sir Bastion himself?"

"Not every man…" Mia thought about the young reporter who had stowed away on the ship. "I am going to go get a bite to eat."

Mia found a book at the door to her room; she glanced down the hall but saw no one.

"*Sweet dreams, little one,*

William"

Mia entered the small bathroom, where there was a small pan of water for her to wash her face. She washed, finding that what she wished for now was a bath. Then she ran water through her hair, knocking down what was left of the tangled mess, pulling it back into a ponytail, and staring at her wet face. She had taken on a lot in a brief time.

Chapter Five

March 1866

Logan Ezekiel looked about the market with no sense of urgency, though the people around him all scattered about running about their business. He watched the young woman as she seemed to float among them, and he wondered how it was that no one seemed to notice her when he couldn't take his eyes off her. He smiled when he thought maybe she, even in a momentary lapse, looked in his direction, hoping it was enough to catch her attention, but she never showed he had. It made his heart ache each time she went about whatever it was she was doing. She was followed by two others, a young man and a much older woman who was wearing clothing not much different from his own. The woman who had caught his attention was near his age, maybe a few years younger, but he was sure she was somewhere in her twenties like him. She wore a dress; it was of dark colors and light-colored trim, and the bottom of the dress had been in the mud so much that it seemed to change all numbers of assorted colors as it swayed.

"Trouble, that one," a man with a gruff voice spoke from behind him. Logan took a moment to look back at Julian Bastion as he took a seat at his side. Julian was accompanied by one of his other brothers, the larger-than-life Mason, as he stood with his arms across his chest, watching the crowd much like he was.

"What's her name?" Logan questioned.

"Mia Penny," Julian replied. "That is her mother at her side, Miss Elizabeth Penny. I'm not sure about the boy's name."

"Miss Elizabeth Penny," he questioned. "The nurse?"

"So, you've heard of her?" he questioned with a smile. Julian was in his army blue uniform; he knew his friend wanted to be a general, and he looked at the medals on his uniform as he rose to command his unit. But it was Julian's looks that often got the attention of others. He was almost chiseled in all his features, a stark

contrast to both of his brothers, the absent Hamilton and the rather hefty Mason.

"I've read articles about her and heard about her daughter." Logan again found himself looking at the woman. "I've heard the stories."

"How do you know her?" Logan questioned as he looked at his companion. He wasn't that familiar with Julian; he was older, and he was much better friends with his brother Hamilton. He watched as the man gritted his teeth and grimaced, almost disapproving of what Logan was thinking. He had only recently found himself spending time with Julian, with Hamilton away overseas dealing with "shipment" issues, which were often thought to mean pirates.

"You should come out with me tonight," Julian stated. His expression became something more neutral as he fidgeted with his freshly ironed jacket.

"I have classes," Logan replied as he again looked forward, trying to find the lovely Mia Penny somewhere in the crowd, but he had lost sight of her.

"Just like my brother, always more worried about your studies…" Julian said as he turned to step in front

of him. "What if I told you that if you came with me this evening, it would increase your chances of meeting Mia Penny?"

This caught Logan's attention as he stood up straight. He wasn't trying to bluster himself to Julian. In fact, he mostly wanted to peak over the taller man's shoulder to get a better look at the crowd, and in doing so, he saw her standing near a fruit stand conversing with the vendor. "You promise she will be there?"

"Oh, she will," Julian said as he turned slightly to look at the object of Logan's affection. "I promise you she will."

"Then missing one night of classes won't hurt," he said with a sly smile as he stepped to one side. His heart raced as he watched her interact with the man, and when she smiled, he thought maybe he had seen the woman of his dreams.

• • •

Just as the sun had gone down, Julian and a couple of others had come to his house. He didn't recognize the two men and thought he knew everyone in the community. They were gruff individuals, and they were dressed down, and almost instantly, Logan felt uncomfortable and out of place, and it was obvious to them. The larger man, a balding man in his forties, gave him a snort of a laugh, watching him climb up on his horse. "Where are we going?" Logan questioned as he looked at Julian, who was no longer dressed in his army attire but looked like something he saw in the travelers' stores that merchants would sell to people who were going to venture west.

"I should have told you before not to look so distinguished where we are going..." Julian said with a half-laugh, looking from Logan to the other two men.

"We'll let him place the bets," the large man said with a hearty laugh. "It may make others think he is a man of knowledge."

"He is going to look like our bloody handler," the other man said with a grin. The two unknown men led off in a gallop, and Julian stayed back, eyeing him up and down.

"Where are we going?" Logan questioned.

"Couple miles outside of town," Julian said as he kicked his horse off into a run.

Logan quickly stumbled about, getting on his painted horse, and followed.

• • •

The path was easy to follow, and torches lit the way the closer they got. When they arrived, he was shocked to see how people looked at him. Ruffians, though he recognized a few of the men who were there and knew they were just like Julian, was dressed down for where they were going. Logan followed to the stable, where he tied his horse up. "What is this, Julian?"

"Fights, boy," the large man said.

"Fights?" Logan gave him a questioning glare.

"Yes, fights," Julian smirked.

"Why would Mia be here? Why did you lie to me," Logan questioned. He saw instantly the two other men looked at Julian and then back to Logan with a serious glare. Neither man spoke, but it was obvious they wanted to say something.

"What is it?" Logan questioned.

"Trust me," Julia replied. "The girl you so admired back in town this morning; she'll be here tonight." Julian walked past him, and Logan rushed to keep up. They reached the circle where two men beat on each other, but he searched the crowd looking for the young woman from the market. The sounds of the two men as they brutalized each other were enough to make Logan wince.

"You lied to me, Julian," Logan stated. He looked at the chalkboard and could see a series of names, but he only recognized Julian's. "You are fighting?"

"I am, and I didn't lie to you," Julian replied as he circled away from Logan. "This isn't like you. Why would you do something so barbaric?"

"You don't know me like you know my brothers, Master Logan," he said as he untied the shawl that was wrapped around his neck and tied it back about his belt loops. "I come here to hone my skills as a fighter. Things the army won't teach me, I learn here. How to win at any cost."

"This is barbaric," Julian said as he glared at the two men, both of which looked like they'd been put through a meat grinder.

"Yes, is it, but then so is war," Julian smirked before he stepped away a few steps and turned back to face him. "If you're thinking of telling my brothers, they already know, and your dear Miss Mia Penny is here, so you only have to look for her. And you won't have to look hard."

Logan stretched, trying to get a better look, but as he looked, he felt more and more that she wasn't here and that Julian was lying to him. There was no way someone as delicate and beautiful as Mia Penny would be here, the daughter of a well-known nurse... He sighed as he eased, and just then, he turned to walk away from the fighting circle.

"Are you looking for someone?" a hooded person said, stepping in front of him, "You look out of place. Looking wealthy here may get you robbed or worse, mister."

Logan tried to look past the hooded figure and stepped to one side, only to have them step in front of them. "I am looking for someone, but I doubt..." His eyes narrowed on the person in front of him, and it was easy to see that the person was a woman. "Who are you?"

"A stranger who knows this isn't the place for you," she said. Her hood was chestnut brown with leather trimmings that came down and engulfed the entirety of the figure in a robe. There was little he could talk about the woman.

"Do I know you?" he questioned.

"You do not, and I don't know you, but much to my surprise tonight, in this barbaric setting, I see you again." She removed her hood, her raven-black hair was tied back into a tight ponytail, and she smiled as she looked at him. Logan felt his knees buckle; she was dressed in men's clothing, and she was even more beautiful in the night's air with the light from the torches dancing off her skin than he had remembered from the market. "I saw you watching me today."

"I'm s-sorry," Logan stuttered. He dug his fingernails into the palm of his hands. He hated that he stuttered. It wasn't something that happened often, but

when he was this nervous. "I mean..." He looked away. "Yes...I was, I'm not sorry for watching you.... I'm sorry if it bothered you. I mean..."

"It didn't bother me," she said with a big smile, looking away from Logan to the circle as the crowd erupted into cheers as the first fight ended.

"I'm Logan," he said, holding his hand out to shake her hand. "Logan Ezekiel."

"I'm Mia," she replied as she shook his hand. Her hand was soft, and Logan could feel his heart beating faster at her touch. "I've seen you around Logan Ezekiel, but I believe this morning is the first time you have noticed me."

"I d-don't believe you," he spurted out without a stutter. "There is no way I could be in your vicinity and not notice someone as beautiful as you." He felt himself blush and started to look away from her. "I'm sorry, I don't mean to be so forward."

He felt her hand on his chin and the slight gesture of a movement to get him to look at her once again. "Don't be sorry," she replied with a large smile, and again, he thought he may collapse just having her so *close and looking so intently into his eyes. "More often than not, you've got your nose stuck in a book or journal or something another of the sort."*

Logan wanted to curse, but he knew it wouldn't be proper. It was true; he rarely ever let anything get in the way of his studies, but he would have thought he'd notice her. "How in all that is holy did I not notice you before today?"

Mia smiled, and Logan felt weak, so weak he thought he would fall over, and he felt her grip tighten on his hand. She seemed to notice as well. Logan forced a smile. He hadn't even realized he was still holding a tight grip on her hand. "I'm sorry," he said, looking at their hands and releasing his grip on hers.

"Don't apologize," she stated. "You're not a competitor, are you? Surely, you are not going to fight in those clothes."

Logan glanced back over his shoulder as two new combatants entered the circle. It was the skinny man who had accompanied them to the area and a man he recognized from the town. The baker's son was having trouble thinking of the man's name, but it was obvious he was in peak physical condition. "No…" Logan replied as he turned back to look at Mia. "It's completely barbaric." He took in her clothing, noticed her bite on her lower lip, and looked away. She was dressed in a remarkably similar fashion to all those around him. He seemed more out of place than anyone. If he hadn't been standing so close to her, he might not even realize it was a woman in baggy clothing. She was there as a competitor. "Oh my…I'm sorry, I didn't mean."

"It's quite all right." Her smile returned. "It is barbaric but beautiful in the same way."

"I'm an idiot. I didn't mean…" He looked back to the circle as the cheers erupted. The baker's son had won, and they were carrying the skinny man from the circle. It was not obvious from the distance if the man was still breathing. Logan looked for Julian but didn't see him.

"Don't be so hard on yourself," she replied. Mia stepped past him, and he turned with her to see the exceptionally large man he had rode in with in the center of the circle, and it was obvious as the entire crowd was looking at her. It was her turn to enter.

Logan grabbed her arm. "Are you sure about this?"

Mia smiled as she pulled her arm free from Logan's grip, her fingernails grazing against his palm for a moment. She didn't do it in a harsh way. "Wish me luck." Logan blushed at her smile as it widened, and he even thought for a moment that he had heard her giggle over the sound of the crowds muttering.

Logan narrowed his eyes, looking at the humungous man, and gritted his teeth before he saw her confident smile. Logan watched as she entered the circle and removed her baggy shirt. The crowd booed. Logan closed his eyes and turned away. He pulled out his watch and flipped it open, watching the second hand as it twirled around the numbers. Repeatedly, he could see it move, but time seemed to stand still to him. He could hear the roars, but all seemed somewhere else. He wanted to turn back and look, but each time he tried, his hand began to shake, and he couldn't move. The crowd erupted as he realized only five minutes had passed, but it was over. Logan didn't turn; he gritted his teeth, and then he felt her hand on his free hand, and he shut the watch and turned. She had a cut on her cheek, and it was obvious she was favoring her ribs with how she stood, but all his worry seemed to disappear as Mia smiled. Logan smiled in a reply of his own. He had only just met her, but he knew then he was head over heels in love.

"I will see you on the morrow at the market?" she questioned as she leaned forward and kissed him on the cheek.

Logan felt his knees buckle under him, but he didn't fall as she watched her turn and walk away. It wasn't until she was completely gone from sight that he realized why he hadn't fallen. Mason stood at his back, holding him up.

"Thank you," Logan said, and Mason only smiled in reply. Logan didn't realize the other Bastion brother was even there.

"Playing with fire with that one," Julian seemed to slither out from behind his much larger brother.

"She's good," Mason said as he turned to face his brother, his broad arms resting on his hips. "Good enough to take even you, brother."

Julian continued to take the tape off his hands as he looked from his brother to Logan. Their eyes met, and Logan could see the intensity in them. The hatred for his newfound love. "She's a feather in a gas lamp. She may float through this life for a bit, but eventually... poof... the flames... they'll catch up with her, and when it is all done, there will be nothing left, and I pray for anyone close to her." Julian's eyes fell on Logan for an uncomfortable moment. He knew what he was trying to say, but Logan didn't care. He had to get to know Mia Penny better!

• • •

For a week, he would see Mia during the day at the market, but the two of them would hardly ever speak until night when he traveled to fight with Julian. He would then only get to speak to her for a little while before she would fight, and every time Mia went into the circle, he would turn his back on the fight, stand with his eyes closed, and listen to the crowd. Not once did he watch her fight, and neither did he want to see any harm happen to her.

The final night, when there were only two competitors remaining, the woman he had so swiftly fallen in love with and the older man he admired even if he would call him a friend, Julian.

He waited for Julian at the same spot he'd met him every night, but he never came. Just when she had given up on him, a horse emerged from the darkness, and he knew it was Mia. "I don't think your friend is coming," she said.

"It doesn't seem like it," Logan replied as he mounted his horse. "Would you like the company?"

"You can escort me to the fights," she replied with a smile of her own.

They had ridden much of the way in silence. It wasn't until he could see the light from the fires that he asked the question that had been burning through him since the first night. "Why do you do it?"

"Because they don't think I can or should," Mia replied. He admired how graceful she seemed to ride on

top of the horse. *"And I know you don't approve, but still, you're here every night, my lone admirer."*

"I'm sure there are others here who admire you and probably fear you," Logan replied.

As they approached the circle, all eyes were on them, and he could see Julian standing in the circle, giving him a disapproving glare. As he looked around, he saw a similar expression that almost everyone had when they looked at them. Logan wasn't sure if it was because of Mia's heritage that they hated her so much or simply because she was a woman.

"You're going to be tempted to watch me fight tonight," Mia dismounted from her horse, and he followed suit. *The two of them circled around in the front and tied off to the nearby rest. Logan would admit he had planned on watching her fight this once, even though he thought it might hurt him more than her.* *"I'm asking you not to."*

"Why?" Logan questioned.

"Because I want you to always look at me the same way you are looking at me now," she leaned up, kissing him for the first time, and he felt his legs almost

give if he hadn't had his hand on the rest bar for the horses he may have fallen. As she pulled away from him, he didn't reply. He only watched as she took off her gloves to reveal her bandaged-up hands and the oversized jacket she handed to him.

He smiled as their eyes met. She didn't. Her expression was all seriousness, and he could see the violence now at the twist of her jaw and the look in her eyes, and his heart skipped. He was equally in love with the woman and afraid of her. Everyone cheered as she entered the circle, and he turned his back on the fight, and for the first time, he heard it all clearly. The oohs and aahs of the fights as they went, he thought he had stopped breathing as he watched his golden watch. It kept going and going for nearly fifteen minutes when the crowd went silent with a gasp. Logan jerked around quickly, looking at Mia as she stood over top of Julian, and all he could see was blood. Julian jerked away, and Logan knew exactly where the man was going. Julian's face was covered with crimson, and he reached his gun and turned, pointing it directly at Mia. Logan stood there with his hands out int front of him. He could see the *hatred in Julian's eyes. Both were eager to strike at the other.*

Chapter Six

Mia stood with her back to the door, waiting to see if she could hear anyone steering anywhere close by. She was going to have to investigate Mister Owen. She took a deep breath and headed the way to the mess hall, walking as silently as she possibly could. It caught her off guard when she stepped into full view of the dining hall table to see Gareth. He smiled the moment their eyes met. He'd heard her and was already poised to launch from the large oak table in her direction as he half stood in a crouched position.

"Is it him?" the voice grumbled. Mia took a step backward, making sure there was no one else in their vicinity, and only eased into a softer stance once he fully sat back down. His mouth was agape, and he stared at her intently. Were her instincts right, and the large, alluring man at the table was the one who was out to kill a little girl? Mia's heart raced to see if she was right. What possible chance could she have against him, unsure if her derringer could put him down

if it wasn't an absolutely perfect shot? "I didn't expect to see anyone up so late."

Two candles on the table lit the room; he was shirtless, and crumbs from bread littered his chest. She walked to the table and took a seat on the opposite side of him, leaning forward. The man was massive, and the difference in size between the two of them was scary, with his chiseled chin and broad shoulders and his hands the size of both of hers. She had never truly realized until now that he was at least three times her size. Towering over the bowl of soup, he smiled and glared at her. Sophia was the equivalent of an ant in comparison.

"Can't sleep… didn't think we should let the soup go to waste," he said, looking up through his thick eye lashes before taking another bite. "Your hair… I prefer the Mohawk," he said, reaching for his cup and taking a big drink. "Want some…?" He reached the cup toward her, and she took it and smelled of the drink, half expecting an alcoholic beverage. It was not. "It's tea…" Gareth said with a laugh between chews. "Helps me focus and stay awake." Not coffee or alcohol, the man was drinking tea, something Mia had never become accustomed to. The only other person who she knew to have a taste for it was her husband. There was steam bellowing from the cup. She wondered if he had boiled it himself.

Mia brought the drink to her lips and took a small sip. It stung her tongue and throat on the way down, but she did not hesitate to push the cup back to him. He let loose a hearty laugh as he took another drink; his laughter seemed to echo throughout the room, and a part of her couldn't help but smile at the sound. "A ship merchant taught me how to make it just right, like pure energy," he swallowed another drink, and Mia only smiled at him as she leaned forward, taking in the scent of his soup. It smelled better than it had earlier, or maybe she was just hungry. "Are you hungry? I noticed you didn't actually get to eat earlier."

Mia looked up from the bowl. For a moment, she caught his eyes narrowed on her cleavage before he met her own, and she swore she saw a blush on his cheeks as he tried to almost be a gentleman. She had skipped through most of her meal as she had spent it studying the people she shared a table with. Gareth did not wait for a reply as he pushed the bowl across the table just in front of her. Mia began to sift through the soup. "I added more pepper to it than what the cook had added." She began by taking a small bite, and her eyes watered. It was spicier than she expected. "We will be in St. Louis tomorrow… late, I think. I heard the captain say

when we set down, a couple will go to town for supplies…
will you ask him if I can go?" Gareth's tone was almost
childlike; he even looked away from her when he asked.
Gareth, after the pause of looking away, brought his eyes back
to her. Most of his features were hard, but his eyes held a
softness about them. He took a big drink of the tea, showing
no effect from the extremely hot liquid.

Mia smiled at the man. Something about his smile
reminded her much of her husband and made her want to run
from the room before any other thought crossed her mind.
Thankfully, the mischievous smile was the end of the
similarities between the two.

Mia watched the man as he leaned back casually in
the tall, backed chair with its copper-colored arms, sturdy
furniture meant to withstand use by rough individuals. The
entire mess hall had a royal feel to it, the long handmade table
with etched carvings of war. Gareth lapped one leg over the
big arm of the chair and watched her as he picked his teeth.
His smile grew ever larger and bolder as he watched her dig
into the soup, almost animal-like. She was hungrier than she
had thought, but there was something more, a hint of
something that was not there with her serving earlier in the
day. "What else did you add to this…?" Mia looked up as she
leaned over her bowl.

"You like?" Gareth questioned with a big smile and a hint of a laugh. "The same man who taught me how to make tea also taught me some other things; the touch of cinnamon can change the taste of even the stalest meal. A little extra pepper from my stash," the man wiped the crumbs from his chest as he looked down and then back to Mia.

The door crept open, Emmitt Frost walked into the room, and almost immediately, Gareth's posture changed. He sat up straight and looked forward at Mia with a slight grin. Frost's normal short-cropped dusty blonde hair was a mess, as was his goatee. His goatee was thick and hid half of his neck. He grinned when he saw them. With a large plate in hand, he approached and took a seat next to Gareth. "I believe it is time to relieve Stone down in the 'dungeon,'" he said with a smile. It was the smile of a man who enjoyed barking orders. Gareth stood, giving Mia the last look with a matching smirk, and left the room.

Mia continued to eat, not looking up at the young man. He never ate with them, and the best she could tell was that he and William Beck were the two crew members who oversaw the Ulysses control cabin. "This grub tastes like two-week-old shit," he said through his mouth full of food. He glared over his bowl at Mia. "It is too hot in this stink hole for a decent, well-cooked meal." He was right about the taste. If you did not get the meal freshly after it was prepared, everything had an almost soiled taste. He stared at her as he chewed, his eyes growing ever impatient.

"Did the brute cut your tongue out or something? I have been told you speak quite… civil?" Mia twisted her head to one side to glare at him, then back to the door, and he started to laugh. "I feel we have gotten off on the wrong foot... and it's been pointed out to me by the captain. This is my fault, and I apologize for this." He extended his hand across the table as if to take hers in his, and the moment she reached to extend the courtesy. He pulled away with a big grin. He again shoveled a couple of bites into his mouth and chewed with his mouth wide. His body moved constantly as he stared at her.

"Spitfire. Beck said you were one, or he believed you were, but I cannot get any sense from the man when he is wearing his damn goggles… he looks a fool." He leaned forward to finish his soup and only looked forward. "But he said at lunch you were paying close attention to everyone… sizing them up. I'm not going to have any trouble with you, am I? Or is there something I don't know about you and your ward?"

Mia had no answer for him. She got up and approached the end of the table opposite the door to the hall where she needed to return. She had kept an eye on the young soldier the entire time until she reached the tray where she placed the bowl, taking her eyes off him for what seemed like only a moment.

Mia turned, and he was there, inches away, and she could feel his warm breath on her neck and chin. "Was not very nice, you know." Pieces of food clung to his goatee.

"What is that?" she questioned with a smile. The two of them were at eye level.

"The pistol in the garter will be hard to retrieve with me already here on top of you." He stepped inward, pushing her back to the table and then another step until there was little breathing room between them.

"Your first mistake." She smiled and leaned her head to one side; he gave her a questioning glare. "Thinking I need a gun… I am asking you to move to one side and let me pass. Or shall I show you again?"

"The only woman on a ship full of men… ignoring your ward..." He smiled and continued to press firmly against her, closing the little gap there. "A tamed savage." He bit his lip, his eyes moved back from her eyes to her cleavage and then back again. He raised his hand up between them, the small four-inch sharp blade with an oak handle. "Hot and sweaty nights on the Ulysses cause some very lucid dreams, and who do you think is frolicking through our dreams? Those small petite breasts, those thin twig-like legs…" He again bit his lower lip and smiled, the knife near her collarbone. "The things I could do to you, and no one on this ship would mind, especially not the captain. He would probably enjoy watching you be broken like a wild animal."

The knife was there and then gone in an instant, pulled from his grip blade first by her right hand. Her left hand grabbed at his crotch until contact was made, and she pulled harshly until he doubled to the floor in pain. She twisted him to his back, knife to his throat, her booted heal pinned his right hand to the floor while the other rested under his body, holding his crotch. "I am far from tame."

"And that would make for two wrongs." She glared up to see Julian standing against his cane. "If you would release the young man, I would appreciate it." Mia removed her boot from his wrist and weight from his body as she took a step back, several until he was free to stand. Frost doubled in pain, leaning against the table. "I would not take pleasure in seeing her broken. She is here to protect my niece, and if I see you so much as look at her… either of them, soldier. I will turn my back the next time while she slits your throat. And I will simply tell your kin you fell from the Ulysses somewhere over the mountains."

The light of the candles flickered off his bronze mask; there was no expression in his eyes or the slightest smile on his lips as he watched Frost limp past and out of sight. "How long were you there?" Mia questioned as she stabbed the small knife into the table.

"Long enough," Julian replied, walked to the table, pulled the knife free, and walked away. Mia did not move from her spot or seem to breathe as he approached the door and stopped turning his head only slightly to look back at her. "You don't like me, Mia Penny, and I don't like you… errors of our youths, but you are under my protection aboard this vessel, and Sophia is under yours as well as mine. I will do all in my power to protect you, and if it means sequestering Frost to a chamber much like Owens, I will do it. I am sorry I put you in the position to fear someone who is supposed to be here as a protector."

Mia took a deep breath. "Mia Ezekiel."

"I'm sorry," Julian said, his head lowered a moment. "Mia Ezekiel, I apologize for what I have just witnessed and all that I haven't, and I will be more vigilant in controlling what happens on my ship." Mia was shocked by what she heard from a man who she knew wished she was dead. "The same can be said for my own attitude and actions. What is in the past is in the past."

Chapter Seven

Mia woke, still dressed from the night before. The last thing she remembered was entering her room after the incident with Frost. She looked around; there was a slight breeze. The morning had come, and with the morning at dawn, the vents of the Ulysses would expel steam, and the walls within the ship themselves chilled from the touch of the outside air. It would not be long after the venting was through the halls that it would again heat to an almost uncomfortable level. It had been said the longer the ship stayed afloat, the more frequent the venting would become. Mia didn't understand why they couldn't remain open at all times but assumed it had something to do with flight stability.

Mia stood and fixed the undercarriage of her dress and then her blouse, including the axe under the vest. She quickly exited the room and approached Hardy's.

Her heart skipped a beat, her thin fingers twirled the key at her neck, and she could see the door cracked open. She rushed forward and into the room. The bed was made, and the young girl was not at her desk. Hardy woke and rose from his place on the floor. "Sophia," she called out, a face full of disbelief and terror. She didn't wait for Hardy to get up. She pulled the door closed behind her. Mia approached the mess hall with caution. She looked at every open door on her way. Terrified, she would find the broken body of the little girl she was supposed to protect. Her mind locked on Gareth, how easily he had slipped up on her the morning of the launch and the ease he could snap the little girl in two if he wished.

Entering the mess hall, she first saw the large six-foot-six man with a bald head. He jerked to attention when he heard her enter. A face full of anger and confusion, she immediately thought of what she'd heard someone say in passing: "Ugly as a bullfrog." Clinton Smith, the cook. He grunted as he returned to cleaning the table in front of him.

"Have you seen Sophia?" she questioned, approaching, staying on the opposite side of the table from him.

There was a pause as he looked from the table, as if he had to think of his answer. "She came with her book." The man pointed to the door in front of him. His voice was barely more than a whisper. There were two doors on the opposite side of the room, one leading to the stairwell going down to the next floor and the other heading to the kitchen. Mia walked forward, trying to be cautious and not look like she was in a mad rush to find the child.

Mia rushed down the stairway until she reached the bottom of the stairs. She entered the first door on the left. It was where she had to be. The room was the Navigation room, as the etched oak sign on the door identified it. She entered, and immediately she saw Sophia sitting beside a table with her nose in the book.

William Beck sat at the table with unusual-looking glasses covering his face. He lifted his head when he heard the door open and pushed a layer of tented glass from the front of another set of glasses. "Think you have been found, child." He glanced at the floor at Sophia, who smiled before turning back to the book in front of her. The man grinned, and it seemed to go from ear to ear. He pulled the second layer of green-tinted glasses back down over the others. The glasses stretched by a band around his bald head, keeping them tightly to his forehead. She had heard Officer Frost speak of unusual "goggles." This must have been what he was speaking of. Her blood boiled as she thought of Frost and how she could allow the situation to come about the way she did.

"Has she been here long?" Mia questioned.

"Maybe an hour. She has been good." He glanced up at her. She could not see his eyes for the thick-tinted goggles.

"She showed up shortly after the first venting this morning, I think the whistle caused by the cold air might have woken her."

"What are those?" she questioned, pointing at the glasses on his head.

"These?" Beck replied with a smile as he took the goggles off and handed them to her. Mia gently pulled them over her eyes, looked through them, and smiled. The words on the pages magnified under the goggles.

"Magnificent," she smiled, pulling them up to her forehead.

"No, no, put them back on and look out there," he said, his voice so gravely and distinct as he turned and pointed out the wide glass panel.

"Did you make these?" she questioned, trying to ignore him as he approached, pushing one lens up and dropping another, and everything lit up. It made her feel as if she could see for miles.

"Me? No, Hamilton did and gave them to me when I told him I was starting to have a tough time reading," Beck replied, "over the past few months, I've added more lenses and stuff to them, but it was all his doing."

Mia gently pulled the glasses off, careful not to let the band catch her ponytail, and handed them back to his eagerly waiting hand. "Do you know him well?" Mia questioned.

"He is a marvelous man, a genius," Beck replied, resting the goggles back on his forehead. Mia smiled; it was not the first time she had heard the man called a "genius." Her husband had often used the same word to describe him.

"Is it true the Ulysses was his work?" Mia questioned, circling until she was close enough to take the seat next to Sophia.

"Him and four others, Daniel Hope is another… this little girl's father." Beck leaned over, taking a better look at the girl before returning to gaze at Mia. "My father, Stephen Beck, and last, Jason Frost, the father of the ship's very own Emmitt." Mia gritted her teeth; she was beginning to realize a little better why certain people were picked for the first voyage of the Ulysses, but the more burning question did it clear them of being the assassin. She looked at Sophia. Mia would not lie; a part of her was hoping Emmitt Frost would be the killer; she could almost taste his blood.

"Can I ask you… why are none of them here?" Mia questioned, curiously eyeing the man as she waited for a reply. She watched as Beck took the goggles from his forehead, wiped the sweat from his scalp, and looked to the book before him, trying to retrieve an acceptable answer.

"Something I don't feel comfortable with talking in front of the little one," he stated with hesitation. "Or in any such place where others may hear," he glanced back to the open door leading to the hall. "It is a conversation we can have after the Ulysses has grounded, and there are fewer ears on the ship to hear."

• • •

Mia led Sophia up the stairway. As they reached the top, Hardy was there starting his descent. "I found the wildflower." Mia smiled. She could see the relief in Hardy's face, which was ghostly white a moment before.

"I think we'll have to be more careful to make sure the locks are secure on our rooms the rest of this journey," Hardy grumbled. But he could not stop smiling as he looked at the girl. "Breakfast is about to be served."

"I'm not hungry," Mia stated. How could she be? It was only a few hours before when she was eating soup with Gareth and Frost.

"It is all right, I'll watch over her for breakfast," Hardy replied.

Mia wanted to finish what she started. She wanted to investigate Christian Owen. He was the most likely suspect, having snuck on board the Ulysses. Hamilton wanted to keep him off this journey for some reason because the young man was right; this was something that should have been recorded.

Mia walked up the hall, stopping at each door until she found one unlocked. It was the one next to hers. She pushed the door open to see it empty. Several journals were sitting on the bed. This was his room, but he was nowhere to be seen. He wasn't in the mess hall; he would almost have to be on the observation deck.

Mia checked each of her weapons as she walked up the steps. She took a long, deep breath as she pushed the door open. It was daylight, but the sun had barely begun to lift upward into the sky. Christian Owen stood leaning against the railing.

Mia noticed he did not look back and paid no attention to her until she was standing beside him on the railing. "Beautiful, isn't it?"

"It is magnificent," she replied. It was. She didn't know where they were high above the mountains, but she knew they would be setting down by the next morning.

The young man looked at her before again looking off into the distance. "I saw Hamilton talking to you but never heard who you were."

"My name is Mia Ezekiel," she replied. She never moved from her position. "And you're Christian Owen, I saw you speaking with Hamilton."

"What is the story here?" he questioned. "What is your connection to the Bastion family or any of the families who thought up this machine?"

"There is none," she lied. She knew her husband was one of Hamilton's best friends.

The young man laughed.

"You're the guardian or co-guardian of young Ms. Hope," he replied. "At least there is a connection. Something got you in the door. I heard whispers when, yet we were still on the ground, you have a history with the captain… will you tell me about it?"

"No," she replied. He was sizing her up as much as she had come to size him up. His clothes are well. He came from wealth. "What paper do you work for?"

"I am freelancing at this time," Owens replied. Mia had been in this world long enough to know it meant he was unemployed. "This will make me famous, the likes of Sir Conan Doyle or Jules Verne." Mia recognized the names as popular authors. "So, the girl, your ward… she is Daniel Hope's daughter?"

Mia sneered at the man. "No." She turned to walk away. It was enough, and she had come to investigate the man but found herself being interrogated in the process. It was unlikely he was there to hurt Sophia. As she reached the door, the breakfast bell sounded.

• • •

Mia had barely made it down the stairs a few paces, and she heard Owen looming over her. He moved swiftly, and he passed her by as they cleared the door at the bottom of the stairway. Mia wasn't truly hungry, but she wanted to spend more time around the others. She wanted to see them in a group setting.

When she arrived, only Julian was there with his eggs, gravy, and sausage. She waited for Owen to get his own before she picked a plate. She had been about halfway through the meal; she could hear Owens fidget in his seat. He wanted to say something, but he was afraid. Kent Hardy and Sophia joined them; it was while they were getting their food that Owen put his journal on the table. Mia looked up at him. He was glaring at Julian.

"Yes?" Julian asked, giving the young man a stern look.

"The mask… you wear it to cover the scar… where did you get the scar?" the young man questioned. The room went silent. Mia fought a smile; she could hear Julian growl as he cleared his mouth with a handkerchief. She felt a little guilty, especially after the confrontation she and Julian had after the Frost situation.

"Young man," he growled. "I will say this once, and the next time, I will fling you over the observation deck myself with no worry of where you land. Do not ask me about my scar again. Or of anything. If I hear you speak in a manner that displeases me, I may consider cutting your fingers off with Ms. Ezekiel's axe; I can only imagine, being a writer, how much such an offense would hurt you." Julian pushed his plate back away from him and stood. He picked up his mask, jacket, and cane and quickly strolled out of the room. It was the second time in less than a day she had heard Julian threaten to throw someone overboard, which had a much different meaning aboard an airship.

Mia looked at Sophia, who was digging into her eggs like she hadn't eaten in days. "It looks like we have found something you like, little wildflower."

Sophia smiled.

"What was wrong with the captain?" Owens questioned.

"Kid, you never ask a veteran about his scars. If he wants you to know the story, he will offer it; otherwise, I would follow his suggestions," Hardy stated.

It was then that Gareth entered the room. He was dressed and smiled. There was the start of a beard this morning, which Mia had not even noticed the night before. His hair was pulled back in a ponytail. The man was clean, as clean as the first morning she had met him. It left her wondering how, when everyone else was miserably sweaty and hot, he looked so refreshed. "Morning, ladies and gentlemen," he nodded, getting a plate of his own.

"You're clean..." Mia blurted out unintentionally.

The man laughed.

"I'm sorry, I didn't mean..."

"The Ulysses has a bath, with warm water and all." He took a seat across from her. He chewed on the bread and smiled. "But if you're like me, a cold bath works wonders aboard this ship."

Mia knew she was blushing. She turned, trying to hide it behind her hands. The man had noticed, but he didn't point it out. She could tell by his small laugh when their eyes met.

"We are landing soon. You may want to get yourself an hour's shut-eye," Gareth stated.

Chapter Eight

The Ulysses had set down miles outside of St. Louis, and four of the crew members left with horses and a wagon that had been stored in the third level of the vessel. Frost, Hardy, Stone, and Smith had left at dawn, and it was a strange feeling looking out from the motionless ship. Mia sat just inside the door and watched Sophia, who sat out in the dirt, still reading her book even though they were outside. Mia had wanted to get a bath of her own after learning about it but never had the time before the others had set off.

"That girl has a thirst for knowledge." She glanced up at William as he stepped out into the sun, and an instant smile graced his face with the sunlight. Even though it was anything but warm outside the vessel, the walls of the ship had a strange silent echo as it sat.

"I thought you would want to go with them to town," Mia said, looking up from her seated position. There was a sense of familiarity with the wilderness around them; it was like where she had been raised.

"I thought it would be wise to stay here, safely inside the vessel." He smiled. "My skin is a little too dark for this territory; situations are still… volatile since the war."

"Guess that explains why Gareth was not allowed to go either," she questioned.

"If you accompany me to the viewing deck, we will set Sophia comfortably in her room. I am sure we have much to discuss." He turned and walked away. She did not want to keep him waiting but hesitated to leave her spot. Even though she had not stepped outside, the smell of the earth so close gave her a freshness she missed. A feeling she had not felt since they left Washington.

• • •

An hour passed before Mia exited the stairway and went out onto the viewing deck. William stood with his back to her; she could see the goggles on his head, even from the door. She approached and leaned against the rail beside him. He had an excited grin on his face as he pulled them from his eyes. She instantly noticed the goggles were different from the ones she had seen him wearing before. These were odd, with several coppers and brace fittings on an immovable lens, the left lenses extended out from the frame a couple of inches further than the right.

He handed her the goggles, and she placed them in front of her eyes without strapping them around her shoulder-length hair. Instantly, she pulled them away. She expected something like the magnifying ones, but it seemed only the extended lens was magnified to an unbelievable degree. "Witchcraft…" she said with a smile, pushing the goggles back in front of her eyes. There was a flash in the right lens now of an assorted color as if it was trying to investigate the dense forest past the trees.

"Maybe. Magic and science can often be confused as the same," he replied with a large smile. She handed the goggles back to him, and he continued to smile.

"Hamilton Bastion is truly the father of everything you see; it was his idea, and most thought him mad," William said, strapping the goggles back to his forehead but keeping them clear of his eyes. "But having a fantastic idea will only take you so far; to progress, he would need others. Others with knowledge, wealth, and authority…"

"And with these men, he got that?" Mia questioned.

"Jason Frost had the ears of Presidents at his tongue; it was he who gave Hamilton the connection to Grant. The government gave him a facility in which to see his dream come to life without questions. All he had to do was pledge its use to Grant and the US Military. With Daniel Hope came wealth. The man had an endless pocket and was more than willing to help his wife's brother. My father, a man of color, was as intelligent as any man, but only Hamilton would dare employ him. The fact is, most still do not know the extent of my father's influence on the development of the ship. Together, they brought everything to the table he needed to build what you see here today." William held his arms out wide.

"Still does not explain why none of the four are on this journey, a brother, two sons, and a daughter, but none of the four…" Mia questioned.

"My father has been dead for two years," he quickly replied, glaring out into the distance. Daniel Hope is missing, two years now since last the little girl's father has been seen."

"Hamilton is alive, and I remember seeing Emmitt speaking to a man who looked like an older version of him," she replied with a long pause... "Two years? Is there a connection between the disappearance of the senior Beck and her father?"

"Rumors are all I know…and a lot of whispers at a rich man's table when the son of an intelligent former slave walks into a room. Some say Daniel killed my father and made it look like an illness; others say it was just old age. Either way, only matters of days separate the death of my father and the last anyone had seen of him."

"Brings us back to the remaining two. What of the eldest Frost?" she questioned.

"The older Frost has dreams of being a senator, or even a future president, a truly self-absorbed man. If he were to one day come to power, it would plunge the nation back into a dark time. There are extreme differences in opinions when you put men of wealth, religion, and politics in a room together, and there is a lot of chance of backstabbing. Each with different views and ideas of how things should be. Neither of the two men have spoken since the ship was completed. It came to a written agreement in letters between the two. Neither would make the maiden journey, but relatives of the four would all be here. This trip was even delayed so they could bring the little girl across the country to make this journey, almost a year between completions to the day we set to the sky."

"A lot of time to wait," Mia stated.

"There are… other issues, a ship of this size with enough quarters to hold nearly thirty men, but yet we are making this journey on less than a skeleton crew," William said with a sly smile. "Each person here was picked because they hold a connection to the four families. Even you, you gave the scar to Julian, but your husband was a close friend of Hamilton's. And you are a warrior at heart and a woman… all three factors are why you were picked to be Sophia's guardian." Mia knew all of this; it was all in Hamilton's letter.

"That leaves three others. What are the connections to the four?" she quickly questioned. The conversation gave her the reasons why they had been chosen.

"Kent Hardy is a lawman, and his connection is through the Hope family…a distant cousin who went west after Daniels's disappearance to try a find him. Rodney Stone, I have known since I was old enough to stand on these legs. He and my father worked side by side in mills all their life. Smith was the Frost family cook all his adult life. And Gareth… I only know he has some connection to the Bastion family."

"So, before the travels, you had never met him?" Mia questioned Gareth.

"You never forget someone of Gareth's… size. I met him twice before, at least I saw him twice before at the Bastion residence. Kent… only the morning of our launch. No more than a day had passed since he arrived back in

Washington, and the Ulysses took to the air. With Sophia and not Daniel no less, it is the first anyone had seen him since he left to find the patriarch, Hope." Mia had hoped a conversation with William Beck would clear up some stuff with the men she was traveling with, but it was raising only more questions.

"Why only crew the Ulysses with men connected with the four men," Mia questioned.

"Since the first day of construction, when it was obvious the Ulysses was not just some wild dream of an educated man that this magnificent ship could one day take to the skies. There were five attempts of sabotage to stop the building. All were failures except minor setbacks," Beck said as he reached into his pocket and pulled out a note. "This was delivered to me shortly after my father's death."

Mia took the note in hand, unfolded it, and began to read it to herself.

"Dear Son,

If you are reading this, I did not recover from this god-forsaken flu. At least the doctor said it was just a fever, but I feel it. It is as if my insides are rotting while I still breathe. I wish for you to come to Washington and speak to Hamilton Bastion. He will be expecting you; I have expressed my wishes for you to take my place on the Ulysses when it is ready. I cannot wait for you to see her; it is everything I could have dreamed of. Even the shell as it currently stands is magnificent.

I do not mean to burden you with the rest, but coming here means I put you in danger. So, I beg you to leave your cousin. I cannot put her in harm's way as well. Forces wish to stop the ship's launch even before it is completed. There have been attempts at slowing our progress, even its destruction. These same people, I believe, are responsible for my current health, so TRUST NO ONE except Hamilton. It is his vision I helped create. He is the only one you can trust.
- your father, Stephen Beck."

Mia folded the letter back and handed it to him; he quickly folded it and put it away. More questions, too many questions. Mia leaned against the railing and looked out over the black forest. She had a lost expression as she tried to figure out the situation in which she was placed. So much she did not know or understand. The one thing she knew primarily was that she could trust no one. Even the man who had told her so much of the history behind the ship she now stood. No one could be trusted; they were all suspects still.

"The people responsible for my father's death did not want to see this ship completed, and here we are, days into our maiden journey. Only people connected to the families were chosen for this trip because one of us would be less likely to try to bring the ship down in flight." He leaned against the rail and looked out as well.

"Do you believe Daniel Hope was responsible for your father's death?" Mia questioned. She never looked at him.

"I never met Mr. Hope. I could have a tough time judging a man I have never met," he quickly replied. "I think if he was not responsible for my father's death, he knows who is, and that is why he disappeared, fearing his own life."

"And that makes Sophia a potential innocent victim of other men's violence before she is even given the right to live a life," Mia questioned. "It is safe to say her mother does not know of such possibilities, or she would have never sent her only child across the country in harm's way."

"Hamilton Bastion brought you for a reason. Maybe he did suspect someone would want to harm the little girl." Mia only smiled as she had been asking the questions herself for days, and she was no closer now than before. Only more questions. "I'll leave you to your thoughts." He turned and walked away. Time seemed to stop until she heard the door shut, and she took a deep breath.

Chapter Nine

Mia had been lying in the bed with her eyes on the ceiling and felt it the moment the Ulysses power-up; the motion of it leaving the ground left an ill feeling in her stomach. She had adjusted to the motion of constantly moving after the first day, but now it was worse than before. She stumbled to her feet and into the small wash area, where she leaned, looking into the mirror. Dark circles enveloped her eyes.

She splashed water across her face and had planned on going back to sleep, but as she walked toward the bed, she noticed an envelope sitting inside the door. She picked it up and noticed the wax seal had not been broken, and the symbol in the wax did not look familiar to her. She gently pulled the envelope open and read the small handwritten letter on the inside.

"Julian…"

Mia looked back at Sophia, who was asleep, or so she thought. She approached the bed, leaning down, whispering near the young girl's ear, "Stay inside, little one, I have to step out for a moment." The young girl shook her head yes, indicating that she was not only awake but understood what her guardian was asking of her.

She heard the key enter the lock and a small sigh when it came open with not so much as a push. Julian stepped into his room; it was the only living quarters on the third floor, separate from all the others. It was also the only one with a window looking out from the Ulysses, and even from her place in the corner, the breeze was refreshing, and she couldn't think about how unfair it was that the room on the guest level did not have windows of their own with how frustratingly hot the inside of the ship got. He slowly unbuttoned his jacket and set it on the back of the chair. He then started to unbutton the sleeves of his shirt. His forearms were scarred in a way that looked like his hands had been caught in a fire. "Come to finish what you started so many years ago?"

Mia had watched him do all of this without making her presence known. Sneaking into his room, standing in wait in the darkest corner from the door. "I have a situation, Mr. Bastion." The words seemed to hang in her throat. He turned to glare at her, hidden in the corner of the room. She knew it had to be him who had slid the letter under his door. After all, it had been from his brother. "I don't trust you, but maybe you're the only one I can trust," she said, holding the envelope open in the air. "And if what you said is true… maybe we can start over and put the past where it belongs."

"Frost will not threaten you again. If he does, you have my permission to do what you must," Julian said. He did not stop his task of unclothing. Slowly, he unbuttoned his shirt and pulled it free from his blue army pants, pulled it from his arms, and hung it with his jacket. His upper body was thin, almost wasting away as she watched his chest heave with each breath. She had thought he'd been faking his illness, but now, seeing him in such vulnerable shape, she knew she was wrong. He had a sickness of some sort.

"Frost is not my problem." She approached him and set the letter on the bed. "I need you to read that. It is the letter from your brother you gave me."

"The letter was for you, not my eyes," Julian quickly stated as he looked at the closed letter. "My dearest brother had made sure I had waited till we were on our way to give you this."

"You need to read it," she said with a frustrated pause. She took a cautious step forward and then stopped again. "Someone on this ship may want to kill Sophia."

Julian gave her a puzzled look, his lips turned down, and his face flushed almost instantly with anger. He peeled the wax seal back open without any more hesitation and opened the letter up wide.

"*Mia Ezekiel,*

My condolences on your husband's extended absence; it would have been him to whom I wished to address this assignment. I am partially responsible for his disappearance from your life; it was upon my wishes he came to Washington those years ago. I meant to write my sorrow sooner, as I spoke with him about bringing you along on the trip, but he told me in person that you were not ready to venture out into the world. And it was I who asked him to travel west for me on the assignment, an assignment he has yet to return from. For this, I do hope you forgive me. One day, the three of us will sit down together for a meal and talk about these days with fond memories of grand adventures.

I know you have been questioning the purpose of your assignment. There hasn't been a minute gone by where I haven't done the same, trying to figure out why anyone would hurt my dear niece. I can only make you a promise and ask for one from you. I promise I will do everything in my power to reunite you with your husband. I only ask that you see Sophia safely in her mother's arms.

Hamilton Bastion
Trust No One!"

Julian looked to the floor as he folded the letter back to its creased position and reached it forward. When Mia took it from his hand, he turned and stepped to the small counter and pulled the bottle from the counter. He said nothing, pulling two small glasses, turning them over, and filling them. He turned to step toward her, eyes still lowered to look at the floor. He handed over the glass and quickly drank down his own before their eyes met. "Where is Sophia now?" Julian questioned. There was a rage in his eyes building as the scar on his forehead seemed to twitch.

"Safely locked in my room," Mia said, putting the glass to her lips and taking a small drink. "The only key to the room is around my neck, and she has promised to open the door for no one but Kent Hardy or me."

"It would be best if you try to keep her there, assure it is the safest place for her without worry," Julian said, reaching to the chair, pulling the shirt back over his arms, and starting to button it back. "Do you know who it is?"

"I only have more questions and few answers… it could be any of them… I do not know them," Mia said, finishing her drink.

"But you are thinking of Frost as your prime suspect," Julian replied as he finished buttoning his shirt.

"How well do you know him?" Mia questioned.

"As well as any captain knows his subservient… I know he follows orders." There was a hollow glare in his eyes, and his lips twitched. Even the tone in his voice was different. He was angry and trying not to show. "But who is to say he isn't following someone else's orders and just waiting to fulfill them."

"What of Gareth? I was told he has some connection to the Bastion family," she had blurted out unwillingly as the thought crossed her mind.

"To the Bastion family, no, to my brother Hamilton, yes," he replied. "I believe he has functioned as a bodyguard for him in the past, which raises the question, why not have Gareth as Sophia's guardian? A question I will dig into. You let me worry about them, and you watch after my dear niece." He pulled his jacket from the chair and did not stop to put it on as he rushed from the room. "There is also our stowaway, Christian Owen, who is positioned mere doors from the child."

"I don't believe he is a threat to her either, but he has been placed so close that if he were," Mia was the one feeling the anger grow now. "Frost placed him in that room… what if they are both in on the conspiracy."

"What of Stone?" Julian questioned.

"Something odd about the man, but he seems decent," Mia said.

"The cook would likely be in cohorts if Frost is our man… he has a connection with the Frost family," Julian stated. He was finished buttoning up his jacket and then plucked the mask off the table where it had been sitting.

"Maybe William Beck?" Mia questioned as she stepped up to the table and poured two more glasses. She could still feel the burning in her chest from the first drink.

"No, Beck wouldn't harm the girl. I can attest to that. He is not a suspect," Julian said as he quickly downed his second drink.

"Stone is connected in some way to the Beck family. Does that mean he is in the clear as well?" She watched as the man seemed to try to catch his breath.

"No, he remains a suspect," Julian responded. "Frost, the cook, Stone, Owen, Gareth… we have our suspect pool, and now we must clear it," Julian responded.

Mia paused, her mouth opened, about to ask him *why the mask*, but as he slowly latched it back in place, she understood for the first time why he wore the mask. Intimidation! The candles reflected off the bronze finish, and she thought she could see hell itself looking back at her in the reflection.

• • •

As Mia came to the hallway leading to the guest area, she came to a sudden stop, bumping into William Beck. She stepped back quickly, surveying the man. "I attempted to bring the young one a book, but neither she nor Kent came to their door," he replied.

"I will give it to her," she wondered just how many books the man had brought aboard the ship. It had occurred to her that if so, many had whispered about Daniel Hope possibly being responsible for the death of Stephen Beck. It would put the man's son at the top of the suspect list. He or Rodney Stone, who had grown up with the man. Despite what Julian had said, Beck was still on the list.

"Thank you," the man said, handing the book over. The man smiled as he walked past. Mia did not move until he had gone from the site.

She turned to go to her room, and as she unlocked it, she saw Sophia tucked into the bed but very much awake. The girl had followed her instructions. Mia smiled. "Enjoying your book?"

The young girl responded with a nod.

"Mr. Beck brought you another one," she held it up for the girl to see. She locked the door behind her and joined the girl in the bed. She set the book on the nightstand with the others and rolled over, watching the girl read. There was a sense of wonderment in her eyes, her slight smile as she read. She again wondered what kind of monster could hurt this child. "Sophia, could I ask you a question." She watched the girl carefully close her book so as not to lose her page, and she nodded a yes. Mia took a deep breath, trying to figure a way to word it so she didn't scare the girl, and for a moment, she thought about being her age and how sometimes, men especially, had made her feel uncomfortable for much different reasons than she was asking but it was still an intuition. "Does anyone aboard the Ulysses…" She paused, looking back in the direction of the door. "Does anyone on this ship make you feel uncomfortable?"

The little girl's smile disappeared with her slight nod just before she spoke.

• • •

Mia sat watching the dinner. A day had passed since her confession to Julian. The frustration grew in her. She could see no difference in the man. He sat stern and unemotional at the end of the table, but his eyes met hers, something they would not do before the conversation. She could see there was respect in his eyes for her; it made her feel uneasy, and this was a man she tried to kill once.

Three were missing from the dinner, Stone, Beck, and Smith. It was unusual to see Frost eating with the rest of the crew; he would normally be on shift inside the Ulysses guidance room. Frost hadn't looked at her, but she could see the red on his pale skin where the knife rested against his flesh. He had rushed through his meal and started to stand, "You are not excused," Julian stated, looking at the man. Frost said nothing. He sat back down, arms at his side like a dog that had been scolded. He said nothing; he just stared forward and made eye contact with no one.

The silence remained for more than five minutes until Kent Hardy got up and returned his plate to the tray. Sophia looked up at Mia, "You can go." Mia knew what the child wanted; she watched as her ward followed Hardy from the room.

A laugh escaped Gareth; he was sitting on the same side of the table as Mia. "Is something funny, boy?" Frost questioned; the two men were sitting close enough that Frost didn't have to move to look at him.

"The dog has been put on a leash," Frost glared at him and then a passing glance toward Julian. Julian stood, pulled a knife, and tossed it to the table between the two men. Mia looked confused. What was happening? What had Julian done?

"Take it outside," he stated, turning and placing the plate in the waiting tray. The last glance was back at Mia before he exited the room the opposite way. Mia then realized how much Julian had manipulated the situation. Did he suspect Frost as well? Was he unleashing Gareth on the much smaller man?

"Looks like I am off the leash," Frost said with a large grin, grabbing the same short knife he had used on her a couple of nights before.

"You don't want to do this," Gareth said, an intense glare up as the man stood and removed his jacket. The man was still smiling. Even with impending violence, he held his large, charming grin.

"Viewing deck, now," Frost stormed off. Gareth pushed the food across the table away from him. He gave Mia a look; he was smiling, but his eyes were filled with something unfamiliar. Anger, she had never seen him angry.

"You don't have to go out there," Mia called out to him as he pushed his chair away from the table. He said nothing and walked past her. He was halfway down the hall before she could even move to follow.

Kent Hardy stood outside his door, arms crossed against him. She glanced, seeing Sophia sitting on his bed. "You can stop this?" Mia questioned.

"I don't believe that is what the captain wants," Kent stated, and Mia thought of Julian. He must want one or both dead. He knows something more than he would tell her. Gareth was a bodyguard to his brother, and he had discovered Frost was indeed the assassin. She had only taken a couple of steps forward when Kent's hand grabbed her upper arm and brought her to a sudden stop. She glared back at him, "I would suggest you stay out of this."

"I have questions," Mia quickly stated, jerking her arm free from the man. Kent was the only one she found herself trusting on this ship. Even if she had come to an understanding with Julian, she still didn't fully trust the man.

"I don't think you want to see what is going to happen out there," Kent stated. She slid the axe down her fingers until she felt the wrapped leather with the small white feather tickling her wrist. Kent took an immediate step back; she had not even realized she had pulled it on him when he grabbed her.

It was then Christian Owen stepped out of his room, catching both of their attention. "Watch him," she glared at the young man. He was at the top of her list, right next to Frost. She rushed to catch the others, not waiting for a reply from Hardy.

Mia reached the viewing deck just as both men were taking their shirts off. She stared attentively at the two men; the air was blistering cold on the outside, such a contrast to the Ulysses.

Mia watched as Frost stabbed the knife into the wooden floor, standing there, a prize for whichever man could get to it first., Frost backed away from the knife, his back to it. He turned quickly after just a few paces, reaching for it. Gareth did not attempt the knife, grabbing at Frost and twirling the much smaller man away from him and the blade. He could have easily picked it up then but didn't. Frost rushed him, leaping into Gareth's midsection and pushing his back to the rail. Mia gasped. For a moment, it looked like the two of them were to tumble over the railing.

"The fool-hearted kid may kill them both without meaning, too." She had expected to see Kent, but the fight had drawn an audience with Beck and Owens. It was William who spoke, his goggles on his forehead. Owen was scribbling in his notebook. She noticed the kid was staring at her hand, the axe still tickling her wrist.

Mia turned her attention back to the fight. The two men wrestled against one another, but Frost could not be pried from Gareth's midsection as he repeatedly ran his shoulder into his ribs. Over and over until Gareth's grip on the side released, the smaller man quickly backed away, bringing a sharp elbow up under Gareth's strong chin. The force of the blow knocked the brute off his feet, sliding down the rail to the floor, holding his chin.

Frost approached the knife with a wink to Mia. She gritted her teeth, and the grip on the axe tightened. She could end this, maybe she should, and take the lashing from Julian for messing up whatever plan he had come up with.

"Don't do it," Beck's gravelly voice said.

Frost walked with a cockiness of a man already victorious. He did not see the large man reach his feet. Just as he bent to pull the dagger free, Gareth was there to shove the small man to the floor, sliding several feet from the wanted weapon. Gareth glared down at the blade but stepped over it toward him. He waited for Frost to reach his feet. The moment he did, a quick handful of hair pulled his face into his thrust knee, and blood splattered the deck.

Seeing Frost's blood did not help Mia's tension. She shuffled in her position sideways, away from the other two men.

A bloodied Frost charged Gareth in the same fashion he did to start the fight, but the bigger man was waiting. A quick step to one side and a well-placed leg tripped the man, causing him to forcefully hit the floor and slide several feet. Mia glanced at Owens, who watched the fight and her at the same time. The kid was too nosey. His attention was as much on her as the fight.

"You mutt," Frost blurted out, reaching for the knife. He pulled it free from the floor as he stood, turning to face Gareth. He weaved in his standing position as he raised a hand, begging for the bigger man to come at him. Gareth only smiled, circling away. "Come, brute." Frost was smiling even with the blood-soaked goatee. It dripped from his face and pooled on the deck below him.

Gareth paced back and forth and then did just as Frost wanted. He charged the knife and dug into his dark skin, missing his ribs. They both slid to the floor. Frost twisted out from under the other's bulky frame and onto his back, where he held an arm around his neck.

The gun went off. She had not even realized Julian had joined them on the deck. His bronzed mask shone brightly in the natural light. "You have worked your aggressions out yet?" he said with a smile. Both men stared at him angrily. Mia stared at him, surprised and probably equally as angry. "Release the man, Frost. Go fix your face before you bleed out. We cannot afford to lose either of you." Mia watched Frost spit blood and saliva onto the floor. He stood.

"Next time," he said, walking backward and looking at Gareth.

Gareth said nothing as the man exited the deck, sat to his knees, and pulled the knife from his side. "I thought you were going to let them kill each other?" Mia questioned.

"The thought crossed my mind. It would have made our mystery easier solved," he said, putting his revolver away and walking into the door, stopping on the top step before he turned back to look at her, "But I thought maybe it would be more entertaining to watch you kill Frost. Gareth was only toying with the man. I've seen the man fight, and he could have broken Frost anytime in the scuffle if he wanted." Just as quickly as he had appeared, Julian was gone.

"What mystery?" Owen questioned if he was staring at her and scribbling something into his notebook.

Mia looked at Beck for a moment, his expression. He was asking himself the same question. Or was it an act? Mia turned just as Gareth approached. He didn't look as angry, holding his side, but his breathing was hard and controlled. "Let's go get you cleaned up," she stared at the wound on his side. As he pulled his hand away, the blood freely rolled out of the long cut.

"Only a scratch," he muttered. Mia had none of it as she stepped in front of the man, axe still in a tight grip; she led him down the stairs into her room.

• • •

Mia finished taping the bandage to his side, and the man radiated heat. He was still fuming from the fight. "Would you have killed him?" she questioned.

Gareth had not looked down on her until then, "Only if he forced me too," he growled. "You hate him as much as me; I can see it in your eyes. No one on board this…this thing likes him. Julian wanted him to teach a lesson and asked me to enrage him to see if he was messing up or saying something out of the way. I'm not entirely sure what game the captain was playing, but I was more than happy to do it." She was right. It was all set up by the captain.

Mia ran her hand down his sweat-soaked chest. Hard; everything about the brute was as solid as the floor beneath her feet. She finished bandaging the wound on his side, the intense grunt from the pain drawing her attention. He was smiling. The same off-to-one-side smile that reminded her of her absent husband. Unlike before, it did not make her want to run away. She bit down on the tip of her tongue as it pressed against her closed lips. His chest rose and fell with each deep, angered breath he took. She glared at the fresh bandage, her fingers still covered in his blood. She leaned into him, not even realizing she was doing so, feeling her body move with each breath he took. Her heart raced as she pushed herself away, looking up into his eyes. She wanted to kiss the man. Before she even realized her thoughts, she felt his lips as she moved up to embrace his chiseled face. Her hand rested on his chest now as she bit down on his lower lip. She wanted to stop.

She stepped away from the man, hitting the nearby table in the movement, a pain she would feel in her lower back for a while. Immediately, her hand went to the pain. She never realized he had moved until he had lifted her from her position, setting her on the table. Mia fell to her back, her head thundered against the table. Both hands went immediately to the jarring echo in her head. She almost didn't feel her legs being lifted onto his arms and the pulling of her undergarments. They were gone before she could even muster a word. She knew what was happening. Her heart raced, feeling one of his strong hands on her leg, his pants, and belt making a clicking sound as they landed on the floor. Mia rose to her elbows, looking into his lust-filled eyes. Again, with his haunting smile. His hands tightly on her legs, he pulled her swiftly to him, sliding her with ease until she was completely engulfed by his shadow.

She tried to speak, but nothing escaped her lips. She didn't know what she wanted to say. Over a year since she was last touched by a man in a wanted manner, the night her husband left for Washington. Despite the similarities in their smiles, Gareth was nothing like Logan. She felt him firsthand on the inside of her thighs. She didn't want him to stop. He was now towering over her; his bulky frame pressed her back against the table. She mumbled again, her hands now firmly against his muscular chest. She was able to breathe easier as he ripped the vest free. With one jerk, all the buttons were gone, exposing the lifted corset and thin black shirt. She could feel him, there on the inside of her leg but not inside, her hips arched from the table against his hips. His large hands jerked her to a sitting position, lips inches apart, and her left hand once again on his chest.

"No," she mumbled, and he smiled. The sharp chill went up to her back. The axe blade pressed into his abdomen; he glanced down between them, taking a step back. She could see the look of shock in his eyes. The smile was gone, but her entire body ached to let him take her.

"I'm sorry," he mumbled cocking his head to one side, his voice shallow and soft, and she could see it in his eyes. He understood why. She felt his confusion, watching him pull his pants back to his hips and latch the belt. A big part of her wanted him to stay. Wanted him. "Sorry," he said, mumbling again as he left the room. She fell back to the table, her free hand on her forehead, the other with a firm, tight grip on the handle of her axe.

Chapter Ten

Mia's head throbbed; the sound of the siren made it worse. She hadn't had anything to drink since she'd been in Julian's room, and that seemed like a lifetime ago with so much that had happened since she told him about the plot to kill his niece. She rolled over; Sophia was at her side. She must have been asleep when Hardy brought the ward to the room so he could sleep as well. She looked over to the corner of the room, half expecting to see the gunslinger sitting there with his hat pulled down over his eyes, but the chair was empty.

She remembered Gareth; she was still flushed thinking about him. She wanted him but made him go away. The horn sounded repeatedly; it was a much different alarm than the one when Owens was found on the ship. *Why was it still going off? Had there been another stowaway found?* She slowly got to her feet, pulling the dress over her head, followed by her vest. She started to button the vest but remembered Gareth had ripped this one from her body and sighed. She tossed it to a corner and got a new one from her closet.

Mia secured the weapons in their rightful places before turning to look at the girl. "Let's go see what the excitement is about, shall we, wildflower?"

Sophia leaped from the bed straight into Mia's arms. Mia packed her down the hall, trying to stay standing, but she could feel the ship. It was dropping and going so fast that her feet would have slid out from under if she hadn't braced them in the doorway. Up the stairs, she held the little girl tight in her arms, her frame too heavy for her, but she pushed through the strain. She released the door to the viewing deck; the wind caught it and slammed it open, and she immediately saw cause for worry. Julian stood with the cane in hand, looking out at the darkness. Streaks of light cut through the sky in front of them.

"Are we crashing?" Mia questioned; she held a tight grip on Sophia's hand as she stood at her side.

Julian smiled. "Landing, this storm came from nowhere. We couldn't fly around it." Rain and hail beat off the ship. "It is going to be a harsh one going to set her down there… we simply can't risk flying through her." Julian pointed to the horizon, and even in the darkness, she could see the open range where there were no trees, "Should delay us no more than a day, two at most. We'll take this chance to ride out to a nearby town and restock some supplies. And Mia… I want you to go with them." She turned to look at Sophia, who was only a step behind her. "You don't have to worry about the little one; she will be by my side the entire time you are gone. I am sending Hardy, Stone, and Gareth out with you."

"No Gareth," Mia quickly proclaimed. Mia could see the curiosity grow in his gaze. "The three of us can manage the resupplies. Besides, it gives me a chance to get to know Stone a little better."

"Settles it, first light the three of you. There is a small settlement, and according to the map, it is a half-day ride from here. You'll go out, resupply, and spend the night coming back at first light. Then we launch back on our way by nightfall the next day." Their eyes met, and she started to argue with the man, but she could see how serious he was, and she knew he'd let nothing happen to Sophia. Despite her hatred of the man and what the note had said, she could trust Julian. As he shifted in his position, she noticed the revolvers on his hips, the first time since she had seen the man wearing a weapon.

● ● ●

The morning was close. Mia sat on the painted horse, which was white and brown in color, and the animal was as ready to run as she was. Mia, like the four horses, could feel the chilly air as it leaked through the cracks of the doors. She wore a black dress without the carriage, which hindered her from sitting on the horse. A black vest latched over the corset and a long sleeve-laced black shirt. The biggest difference from her everyday wear was the hood and the gloves kept her face hidden from anyone who would see her first. On the inside of her heavy jacket, the revolver pushed awkwardly on her hip. She wasn't the best shot in the world, but if she had time to take aim, she was more than adequate.

Rodney Stone, the largest of all the men, sat upon the strongest horse, the black stud tallest of the four, but the man still had to look up to look others in the eye. He and Hardy dressed similarly in long black dusters over brown pants, shirt, and vest, each of the three in worn boots, long past their usefulness. He seemed oddly comfortable high on the horse, as did Hardy.

Kent Hardy even smiled as he mounted his tall white horse. It was the first time Mia had seen the expression when he wasn't with Sophia. He would have another horse of similar color and features trailing behind him on their way to the settlement. Mia wondered why Julian had wanted both her and Hardy to go.

William Beck's goggles were on his forehead, and he walked into the room with a smile, hands on his hips as he approached the door. With just a push, the large mechanical gears on the two sides of the room started to shift and move. The horses, nervous from the loud sounds, moved with tension as the doors to the cargo area of the Ulysses slowly opened. Mia smiled with the cool air flushed into the hold unhindered by the large door. "We will be looking for you midday tomorrow," Beck called out. Hardy was first, but Mia kept her horse at pace with the others. They both seemed to have equal experience of riding. Stone was not far behind.

• • •

They rode for most of the day until they reached a point, and immediately, they brought the horses to a crawl. They could see the small mining town in the distance. The rain had slowed to only a drizzle, but the clouds overhead rumbled something fiercer to come. Hardy pulled his horse to a stop, looking in the direction of the town, still a quarter of a mile away. "What is it?" Stone questioned from the back of the

145

group. There had been hardly anything spoken between the trio for the entirety of the ride.

Mia pulled her hood from around her head and let it rest on her shoulders. "No smoke," she said as she looked at Hardy, who nodded.

"And that means…?" Stone questioned.

"No smoke, no fire. I see fifteen buildings, homes, a church, a common store, and no smoke from a single stack," Hardy stated, reaching and pulling one of his pistols and letting it rest in his hand. It sat on his upper leg, still partially hidden by his coat.

Mia pushed her vest open just a bit so the axe was easily accessible and pushed the coat back so she could pull the revolver with ease if she needed it. "So, we are expecting trouble," Stone questioned, bringing his horse up beside the others.

Hardy and Mia continued to look toward the small town. "We are expecting to find an abandoned town at best."

"And worst?" Stone quickly questioned.

"Bodies," Mia said, giving a slight kick to the sides of her horse to get it started. "Lots of dead bodies." Hardy did the same, getting the horse moving to let the reigns of the other horse trail behind. Mia kept a careful look at the sky for carrion but saw none and nothing on the small trail, which seemed out of place to her.

"Great," he muttered as he reached and grabbed the reigns of the free-standing horse who Hardy had released. "One of you wouldn't happen to have an extra gun, would you?" He kicked the horses up to try and catch up with them. Mia smirked; it was hard to believe Stone had come all this way before asking for a weapon of any sort. She twisted and looked back at the man. "What? I don't like guns."

• • •

The closer they got to the small town, the slower they traveled, keeping a look both forward and to the ground in front of them. "Been riders in here since yesterday," Hardy stated, Mia was busy watching the wilderness around them. "Looks like three, maybe four, in and out of town at least twice since the hard rains, so late last night, possibly raiders."

The road sank before them, and then a small slope upward, and they came to the first building, a small white-painted church. It was the only painted building in the eyeshot, and it looked the cleanest of them all. A large wood cross stood beside the door nailed to the wall. Mia guided her horse

between the two men until she brought it to a stop and twisted
her leg off. Her boots sunk into the mud, and the bottom of the
dress soaked to the wet ground. "Where are you going?"
Hardy questioned.

"Bad time for praying," Stone called out.

"Never a bad time for prayer, no matter who you pray
to," Hardy replied, and Mia looked back at him.

Mia kept her pace, walking up the two steps to the
small porch, and pushed the doors inward. Five rows of
benches, velvet-covered cushions on both sides of the
walkway. The church was not very wide, but between the two,
there was enough to house twenty worshippers. Mia walked
the aisle slowly, taking a moment to glance at the benches.
She stopped at the front row, looking back. The door still hung
open, and she could see her restrained horse outside. Mia
stepped up onto the small stage area, and behind the podium,
the church was empty. Still, with a tight grip on the revolver,
she rushed back outside. She had stepped back into the light;
the rain was beginning to pick up, and she saw Stone, the
small house on the opposite side of the road.

Mia stepped down; she saw Hardy still high on his
horse a few houses down in the middle of the street. She
rushed to the building closest to the church, where there was a
small store inside. The floor was covered with debris from

shelves turned over and shattered wood. Nothing else remained. After a quick check of the back storeroom, she rushed back outside. Stone had just exited the first small home; she could see the look of shock on his face. Pale as a ghost, even through his beard and hair, his eyes were wide. He sat on the porch, Mia moved across the road, and he glanced up at her just as she stepped up on the porch. "You don't want to go in there," he muttered.

Mia never hesitated to walk in the door. There was no smell, but she immediately saw the black stains on the floor where blood had pooled and dried away. She slowly paced to the back room and saw the decaying body of a young man, his hand across his stomach, his right hand in a position where it had been raised in waiting with a pistol. If not for the clothing, it would be hard to tell it was even a man lying before her. She took a deep breath before turning away. She almost wished she could say this was the worst thing she had ever seen. But she had seen a lot in her youth.

Mia made haste out of the cabin; Stone still sat on the small porch with his head in his hands like a statue she had left before entering. "Come on." She grazed her hand on his shoulder. It was then she saw Hardy on the same side of the road as they were. He waited outside a door; she walked fast past three homes before she was at his side in front of a saloon. "Church and store are empty; we are not going to find any supplies here."

"What do you think happened here?" Stone questioned. He was out of breath, still gasping from what he witnessed more so than the run to catch them.

Hardy lifted his hand in the air and opened it. The braced shell hulls fell to the floor at his feet. "Shoot out of some sort." Pistol still tightly gripped in his other hand, he stepped into the saloon.

It was hard to look away from the body when they entered. Hung from the second-story ceiling, the near-skeletal corpse waved at them from the banister, making a small, near-silent crunching sound each time the wind pushed it into the railing. The figure, also a man, wore no boots or shirt, only pants hanging to the frame by the belt dug into the rotting flesh.

"Maybe we should head back to the Ulysses," Stone stated, staring at the figure. Hardy walked toward the saloon's bar. Around the back, he dug for a moment, and they could hear cracking glass under his boots. He lifted the bottle, pulled the cork, and watched as only dust escaped.

"Be dark in a couple of hours. If you want to make your way back to the Ulysses, you are more than welcome to try," Hardy said as he continued to dig through bottles and glass behind the bar.

"Shouldn't we? We are not going to find anything useful here," Stone stated.

Mia walked forward until she got to the stairs and slowly walked up to them with a hand on the soft sanded banister. She did not speak until she reached the top of the stairs. "You won't make it back to the Ulysses if you leave now."

Stone looked puzzled as they glared back and forth between them, "What aren't you two telling me?"

"The tracks go through the center of town. Someone travels through here almost daily," Hardy said. He glanced upward toward Mia.

"Watching for travelers to murder and rob," Mia replied, and she could see the shock on Stone's face.

"They likely ran this town when it was active, and the local mines were profitable when they ran dry and most law-abiding citizens gave and left, then they took over until they ran the rest out or killed them," Hardy said he was continuing to open empty bottles. "And they probably already know we are here."

"What do you mean," Stone said. He jumped backward as the hanging body fell to the floor below. Mia stood with her axe at the top, looking down at them.

"We should search the rest of the homes before dark and be ready for a long night," she stated.

"And get the horses out of sight," Hardy said. Both were looking at Stone, who still seemed puzzled.

"Fine." He turned and marched out of the saloon.

• • •

Mia spent a moment looking through the upstairs room before she walked down the steps. Hardy had placed both of his pistols on the bar and was cleaning them. "When do you think they will come?" she still held the axe in one hand, and in the other, she packed something new, a five-foot-long decorated spear.

"Before sundown," Hardy replied. "You any good with that thing?" He looked at the long spear and watched as she flipped it where it rested in the palm of her hand and threw it. It stuck in the large beam near Hardy.

"Probably better with it than the pistol, at least for an initial assault." She smiled. She had found the spear hanging over the top of a bed in one of the upstairs rooms. "Still, we will be outgunned."

"If I can't talk our way out of this, I want you to be upstairs here. Use the spear if you can, if not… I want you to slip out the back and make your way back to the Ulysses," Hardy replied. He placed the first pistol back in its holster. "It will be harder for them to track you alone than the three of us, plus I'll keep them distracted for as long as I can."

"You will get no argument from me," Mia said with an eerie, suggestive smile. "I am not so sure Stone will enjoy the idea of making a last stand here."

"That is why we are not going to tell him," He finished checking the sights on his remaining gun. "I want you to get back to the Ulysses and keep Sophia at your side. Get her to Lana in California."

"Lana?" Mia questioned how she set the axe to the bar and used both hands to pull the spear from the wood.

Mia smiled, placing the spear on the counter, and placed the axe back inside her jacket. His lips parted, but there was hesitation. The way he had said the name, there was more meaning to it. "Sophia's mother." He holstered his last gun, then pulled his jacket close as he looked at her.

"I never… no one has even said her name to me until now," Mia said. "You've been Sophia's guardian for a while, haven't you?"

"Sophia is a smart, uncomplicated child, and she took to you," he said. "Now it is my job to get you back to her so you can get her safely back to her mother and you back to your husband." Mia smiled; it was then Stone entered the saloon. Mia was slightly confused by the exchange.

"We have a rider," he said, winded. Mia picked up the spear and started up the stairs, "where did you get that?" Stone questioned but got no answer. She circled up and around the stairway, stopping at a window where she could see the center of the town outside.

Hardy walked to the middle of the street, wrapped in his jacket, where both of his guns hung free and ready to draw. The rider approached from the same direction they had entered the town; he rode a large black horse at a trot until he was only a few feet from Hardy. He took off his hat, an older man in his fifties with a naturally balding head and square-jawed face. He smiled as he looked around. "You alone, cowboy?" He questioned. He was looking around for others; Stone was still inside the saloon, out of sight as well.

"Just passing through," Hardy replied.

From Mia's position, she could see at least two riders coming from behind him, one wearing a hat, and she could tell little about him. The third did not, a young man in his twenties with shaggy brown hair and a clean-shaven face. "Is that a fact?" the older man questioned, still looking toward the saloon.

"Two more with him, paw," the one without a hat called out. "A short fat man and a savage, I saw her clear as day… she may have been dressed white, but she was Sioux, maybe Shawnee."

"You are riding with a savage cowboy?" the man questioned with a big grin. "Brave soul, you just asking to die in your sleep," he leaned forward on his horse, looking down on Hardy, who did not as much as a grin.

"We don't want any trouble, just passing through is all," Hardy said.

"My boy hears and sees some strange lights at night east of here. We told him it was just some lost cowboy's fire… was that your fire he saw last night?" the old man questioned, sitting up straight on the horse and looking toward the saloon.

"It is possible," he quickly replied. "We thought we might ride out the approaching storms here for a night or two, looking for a warm drink, but it seems we came too late."

"I'd say," the old man said with a big smile. He reached into his saddle bag, pulled out a bottle, and tossed it to Hardy. The entire time, his hand twitched, wanting to go for his gun, but he didn't. "Has a nasty bite to it, but will warm your belly." Hardy smiled, pulling the cork, and brought it to his lips but did not drink, allowing the liquid to touch only his lips, making it seem he did. He bit his lip as he closed the bottle and tossed it back. The old man placed it back in its saddle bag. "I'd like to meet this savage of yours." It was then two more riders approached from his back, both in dusty gear similar to the others.

"Just the three of them, boss," the one said. He lifted his hat off his eyes.

"See, we are the friendly sort. You can trust us," the old man stated as he rose and pointed at the other Indian.

"Just move along, and we will go from here come morning," Hardy stated. He turned in his tracks to get a better look at the four men behind him.

"You are not being a very friendly cowboy," the older man said.

Mia never heard him, just the hammer of the pistol as it pulled back into a firing position. She turned to see a sixth man, larger than Stone but taller than her. "Now, little lady, be a nice little savage and hand over the blade." Mia tossed the axe and spear to his feet. "Now come with me." The man shifted, not letting Mia get close to him. Just as he stepped out, she turned, and he lifted the pistol. If he had been just a couple steps closer, she'd been able to strike. "Don't." Mia gritted her teeth as she started down the steps and out the door into the rain as it began to come down harder.

Mia was the first out the door, followed by Stone, both hands in the air as they approached Hardy. The older man smiled when he saw them and immediately shifted off his horse. "Now, was that so hard?" Hardy glared at Mia.

"Look at the size of that one... hey Blackfoot, what was it you used to do to your enemies?" the youngest man questioned as he pointed at Stone.

"Tie them to trees and split their guts for the ants and vultures to feed on while they still breathed," the Indian called out. The other men smiled, but he didn't. He glared at Mia. "Boss, she is Cherokee..."

"See, Blackfoot here has been with us... well, longer than my son. And one thing I know about him is that he hates all of you other savages except his kind." Blackfoot shifted off the horse, and the knife sliding could be heard by all as he pulled it out.

"She had these, bosses." The man who had snuck up on Mia tossed her axe and the spear to the ground between them.

"My, aren't you a pretty little thing," the old man said with a smile, a firm grip on her chin, turning her face from one side to the next. "What do you intend to do with her, Blackfoot?" The old man smiled as he looked at the approaching man. "If you can stomach her, maybe it's time you settle down from your wicked ways and have a bride."

The large Blackfoot said nothing; his long black hair came free and reached near his waist as he tossed his hat to the wet ground. He glared at Mia, whose fists clenched tighter as she looked from the approaching man to Hardy. There was no fear in Mia's eyes as she looked at her companion. Hardy gave only a slightly noticeable nod.

The moment the older man released his grip to her chin, the tip of her gun was to his jaw. Simultaneously, she and Hardy fired. The bullet ripped through the smiling jaw of the older man, on one side and out the other side of his mouth. The man twirled in pain away from her, grabbing at his jaw. In a second and third shot, both the large man and Blackfoot were shot dead by Hardy.

Other shots rang out as everyone scattered from the road, a haze of mud, blood, and gunfire. Mia had taken only a moment to lift her axe from the ground before she ran, putting the older man's horse between her and the others. "…oot at itch…" the old man was trying to yell out, not knowing from his position she had placed him between her and the others. He sat on his knees, holding his face in pain; the man shook violently as blood covered his hands.

She smacked the horse and ran sliding behind the old man and twisted his upper body, placing the blade of the small axe to his throat. She looked around, and only the three men remained. Even Hardy and Stone had scattered from sight. "Pah, are you okay?" the youngest of the men called out.

"Does he look all right?" Mia questioned. She tried to keep him firmly between her and the three gunmen.

"Young savage, I'm going to cut you ear to ear," the young man called out. One of the men circled perfectly in front of the saloon, and two gunshots echoed from the inside. The man fell forward dead.

"Don't come any closer." She pressed the blade up into the skin until blood began to run down the sharp edge.

"There doesn't have to be any more bloodshed here today," Hardy stepped out, both guns aimed at the remaining two men. "You can take your father and return home. He may even live if you get him some help quickly."

"Do you think…?"

Hardy shot again, and the only remaining man standing was the son. He looked at the man on the ground beside him and immediately dropped his pistol. "Your choice, kid," Hardy stepped out into the mud.

Mia quickly stepped away, turning her back to them as she took several deep breaths, adrenaline pumping her knuckles white from the tight grip on the axe. She had turned back just in time to see the older of the two reach for his holster. How had she missed disarming him before? There was no hesitation as the axe sang as it twirled through the air, ending its song in the back of his skull.

Two shots rang. Mia hadn't seen the young man move, but he was now lying dead in the muck, and she sighed. He holstered it and turned to look at Mia. She had dropped to her knees. The old man was the first person she had ever killed. It felt wrong. Tears ran down her face as she stared coldly at the man lying face down in the mud with her weapon cleaved into the back of his head.

"Are you hit?" Hardy questioned. It was at this time Stone came from the saloon. Mia said nothing and could not see the gunslinger as he covered his left shoulder and his shirt stained with blood. "Mia? Are you hit?"

As if being woken from a deep sleep, she looked around and then at the man speaking, "What?" she questioned, pushing her way back to a standing position.

"He asked if you were hit," Stone questioned.

She took a moment as if to look for wounds, even though she would have known. Her hands shook, but there were no other wounds besides skinned knees. "No, are you all right?"

"Clean through," he said, walking across the road. The old man's horse stood on the walkway in front of a home. He grabbed the reigns, pulled it to him, and reached into the saddle bag for the bottle of liquor. "I'll live."
He took his mouth, pulling the cork and spitting it out. He grimaced in pain as he poured the strong drink over his shoulder and then took a quick drink of his own. "Stone, since we did all the work…" He turned and walked out into the road. Taking a small drink, he stepped up beside Mia, handing her the bottle. "Drink, it'll calm the nerves," her hands were visibly shaking as she stared down at the old, balding man. "You get to search the bodies for usable stuff, take all their weapons." He reached down and pulled the axe from his skull with a squeal of bone and brain as it came free. He wiped it clean on his pants and turned back to Mia with the weapon reached out. "You had no choice."

"I thought I could manage this…" She took the axe by the head, and despite Hardy's quick attempt, blood and hair still clung to the blade.

"You're stronger than you think," Hardy said as he took the bottle from her other hand. She still had not taken a drink. "The first man I ever killed was just a year ago." He took a drink from the bottle and then placed it back in her hand. He waved his hand in front of her face, "You were willing to kill Frost, and this is no different. These people would have killed us… they fully intended to kill us. You saw one body in the saloon and the other in the house. And I am sure there are others here…" She stared into Hardy's eyes. Only coldness stared back at her. She did not want that for herself. Maybe once she was meant for this, but no more. "They intended on killing us and maybe much worse." She knew what he referred to.

"I can't…"

"Take a drink. It'll numb the thoughts," he stated. He lifted the bottle still in her hand to her lips, and she took a big drink. "It is easier to get through this than people say," he took the bottle and another drink of his own, and he lifted the bottle. There was only one last drink. He handed the bottle to her and walked away toward the saloon.

He stopped at the steps and looked at Stone, who was clearing out the pockets of the bodies. He only paused for a moment, another glance back to Mia before he entered the saloon. She finished off the drink and tossed the empty bottle to the body in front of her. She had not even realized it had stopped raining, and the sky above had cleared even though the darkness still loomed for the night.

It was several hours after dark before Mia entered the saloon. She was surprised to find Stone asleep just inside the door. Huddled on the floor with an old, musty blanket pulled tightly over him, not a sound escaped the man as his chest rose and fell. Hardy sat with his hat pulled down over his eyes, boots propped up on a table. He had lifted the hat for a moment when she entered; it was obvious she had been crying.

His shoulder had an old shirt wrapped tightly around it to hide the wound. "Are you okay?" he questioned as she took a seat across from him and set the axe on the table. It was spotless now, the string once holding the small white feather now around her neck hanging just above her collar bone. Her face flushed red from crying, and four long, thin scratches ran down the side of her face, self-inflicted.

Her hands sat beside the axe, still shaking, and wore a harsh redness, as if the blade were not the only thing she tried to scrub clean. She bit down on her lower lip and glanced back at Stone, still hibernating on the cold floor. "The first man I killed was luck, plain and simple. He was a stumbling drunk and still faster than me. He shot three feet in front of me before I even got my gun from my holster. He fully intended to kill me, and I had no choice. I was sick for days, vomited my gut up until there was nothing more inside… and then it continued for two days of pure gut-wrenching pain and sickness. The second man was much of the same."

Hardy pulled his legs from the table and sat straight, reaching into his vest and pulling a small bottle, only a few drinks left in the bottom. "You never hesitated in pulling the trigger when you saw the opening, but you did it knowing it would not kill him, a clean shot through both sides of his mouth. You gave him every opportunity to walk away from here today. The moment he went for his gun, he lost his choice. And you lost yours." He set the bottle only an inch from her hand. "All those others on the Ulysses see the woman who has a reputation for violence because of how you were raised. They never saw you as Mia, Little Feather." He glared at the small white feather around her neck. "That is what Logan preferred to call you, isn't it?"

Mia gave him a questioning glare; how did he know that? Of all things, how did he know about the name Little

Feather? She could not put it into words; her lip and chin could only quiver in anticipation, but no words escaped.

He only let the bottle sit for a moment as he reached and pulled it away, pulling the cork with his mouth and spitting it to the floor before he lifted it in the air, looking at her. "To whom you are today, whether you want to believe it or not, Mia Ezekiel, you are a much more dangerous woman than anyone knows, and trust me, they think you are quite deadly." He took a drink and then set it back down in front of her with a final drink, waiting to taste her lips.

Chapter Eleven

November 1868

It was an hour past dark when the carriage pulled by a team of five horses thundered up the white cobblestone drive. It was hard to tell where the hand-placed rock ended and the near-foot-tall snow started. The reign bearer on the front of the carriage, bundled in three to four layers of clothing, pulled on the reigns to stop. If he said a word, it was so chilled and low that no one heard the yelp. Only the crashing and grunting of the horses as they came to a stop, almost immediately he tied the reigns off and jumped to the harsh surface below.

He rushed to the back door of the carriage. As he opened the door, a large man of six-foot-two bundled for warmth was quick to the ground beside him. By the time the fifth and last person exited the carriage, the doors of the large home had opened.

Logan Ezekiel wiped his hands clean as he stepped out into the brisk cold, his brown hair shaggy and covering his ears and the back of his neck from the cold. "Afternoon, gentlemen," he said as he rushed down the steps to meet the first of them.

Mason Bastion was busy looking at the cobblestone drive. "A lot of challenging work went into this drive."

"And a pretty little penny it cost, too," Logan said as he shook his hand feverishly, his white sleeves rolled up to his elbows.

"I probably could have done it cheaper," he said with a big grin, his grip tight on the other man's hand until he saw the grimace of pain on his face, and then he released his grip with a big hearty grin.

"So, I take it business is good?" Logan said as he addressed his wounded hand and ego. Mason was bigger than he last remembered. He had heard the man had gone into the business of building roads when he left the army.

"It provides," he said with a smile. He turned just as a small woman took her arm into his. The woman was dressed in an elegantly long red dress with lavishly large pearls distracting from her deep cleavage.

"This must be the new Mrs. Bastion. I hope the gift reached you in time, a specially made saber just for your old friend. I am sorry I could not attend your wedding in person," Logan said with a smile. He gave a slight bow to the woman. Her large blonde hair distracted from her face, and she returned his smile and bow.

"This is my wife, Macy, and this is Viva," Mason said. Another woman was dressed similarly. "Macy's sister. I thought we might make an honest man out of you before our visit was through." Logan smiled and raised his left hand, and the golden band glistened even in the dim light outside the home. "When?"

"July," Logan replied with a big smile. "It was something of short notice."

"Congratulations, my friend. Do we know her?" Mason questioned.

"You do indeed, but we'll discuss that later," Logan quickly replied. He looked to the remaining two men.

"I'd like to introduce you to the Flannery brothers, Thomas and Sawyer. They are along for security purposes," Mason replied. Both men wore similar gunslinger-like outfits, vests with gun belts, hats, and long duster jackets. They were equally fit with thin, wiry frames and strong jaws.

"I thought your brother Hamilton would make the trip with you," Logan questioned. He glared at the carriage as the man who had opened the door was pulling luggage from the top of the structure and carefully sitting it down. *"And why the security?"*

"One and the same old friend, Hamilton, was called off to Washington, and there has been some talk of threats against my father's new bid to run for Senate. And just a precaution, a conversation I am sure would be better taken up inside in front of a fire and a warm drink," Mason said with a heartily big grin.

"Where are my manners?" Logan said. He put the rag in his pocket and moved to one side to allow the others inside out of the cold.

The group had made their way to the living area of the large home; several large couches littered the room where the woman had made their sitting side by side. The two gunfighters stood by the door while the others stood near the kitchen area. Logan walked into the room, rolling his sleeves down. "I have a maid settling your quarters, and they will be ready momentarily. So, tell me, Mason, why has Hamilton ventured off to Washington?"

"You know my brother; he has a wild idea he is trying to get off the ground. He is hoping to make some connections within the city to help him see it come to fruit. It is a year or two from getting started, but I cannot explain the craziness in which he has dreamed up. It would be best if you travel to Washington to see with your own eyes when the weather breaks." Mason stood with his back to the fire. He, like the two brothers, was armed with two pistols on his side, more visible now with his large jacket off.

"I assure you, there will be no attempts on your life in my home. You can put your weapons away," Logan said. He had pulled his own vest on to look more in place with the others.

"Still no fan of the gun, Logan?" Mason questioned with a big smile.

"They have their place. I have become quite the shot myself," he said with a smile. The two brothers could be heard with their wanted laughter as they looked at the man.

"You carry yourself differently from the last I saw you, Logan. Married life has done you well," Mason said with a cheery smile. *"So where is she?"*

"Sleeping," he said with a reply. *"Early to bed sort. There is plenty of time for that tomorrow. Let's get you settled in."* He turned and left the room, and they all followed.

Morning came, and the smell of fresh food filled the home. Mason walked down the stairs to find Logan sitting as he poked at the roaring fire. "I was wondering

if you were going to sleep the day away, old friend,"
Logan questioned.

"Days of rising early for soldiers work have long since passed, my friend. Now I wake when I want," he said with a hearty laugh.

"Walk with me," Logan said as he stood. He approached the door and pulled his jacket from a nearby free-standing rack. He wrapped it around him and slogged out into the cold, brisk morning with Mason on his heels.

They walked in silence until they were far from the house. Walking in the high snow took a lot out of both the men as they had avoided the freshly cleaned trail to the bar and walked to the old willow tree. "There is something you are keeping from me, Logan Ezekiel, but I cannot tell what it is."

"Been almost two years since I last saw you and your brothers. I spent a year of it back home before I felt safe enough to come back. Tell me, how is Julian?" Logan questioned.

"Eh, the man is not well," Mason said as he picked his feet up from the snow and walked toward the tree.

"Has he fallen ill?" Logan questioned.

"Physically, he is fine. It is his head where the sickness lies," Mason replied. "When we returned from..." He paused to look off in the distance before he accepted what he was saying, "his scar proved too much for the Hope girl. She would have nothing to do with him. He was court marshaled for killing a man after that... had a hearing and everything. It was then found to have been a defensive action; I am still not sure if it was so. He killed the man in a blind rage, and I'm his own brother to say such a thing. He has retired since; he does not eat enough to keep him physically stable. He has taken to wearing a bronzed ball mask to hide the scar that woman gave him..." Mason turned slowly to look at Logan. "What happened to her, Logan?" he questioned with an intent glare.

It was then two women walked from the barn near them, side by side in their pale blue dresses with their long trains dragging behind on the cleared path. Both had hair as dark as night, but Mason knew immediately one of them was the very woman he was just asking about. "She still…" He could see Mason's hand twitch, and before his old friend could pull his weapon, Logan had pulled his own, getting the other man's attention. He raised an eyebrow before looking at the gun and then back across the field at the two women.

"I would ask you to not point your weapon at my darling wife," Logan said, a face full of serious intentions.

Mason moved his hand away from his gun and laughed, which both women heard, and turned to look at the situation. "I wanted to tell you," Logan said with a blank stare. "I knew the reaction if you or Julian had heard the news from anyone but me, so I kept it secret."

"You fool of a romantic," Mason turned to face him.

"…so maybe I am a foolish romantic," he replied. He glared across the small distance at his wife, and they shared a smile.

"No maybe to it," Mason said with a laugh. He was now standing with his body full to him and held out

his hands. "No ill intentions from here forth, friend. Congratulations are truly in order. You tamed one who we thought you would have to put down." He grinned as they shook a normal handshake, unlike the one the night before.

"Heh, she is far from tame, my friend, I promise you, but she is no threat to you or anyone else," Logan said with a smile and laugh.

"I can see this is going to be anything but a dull few days' visit," Mason said with a grin, "Wait till my dear wife meets yours. I recanted tales of that day, course… I may have exaggerated," he said with a laugh as he marched forward toward the two women. Logan was only a step behind his pistol, which was still nearby.

Like a marching rhino, Mason did not stop until he was close enough to touch the two women. He reached for her hand. "It is an honor to meet you, Mrs. Ezekiel."

"Mia," the other woman called out.

"It is an honor to meet you, Mia Ezekiel," he said as he raised her hand to his bowing lips. "And you are?" He glared at the other woman. Both wore nearly

identical dresses, and she, too, was in her early twenties, but her skin was pale as the snow at their feet. A small chain necklace circled her throat down into her modest chest.

"This is Jean," Logan stated at Mason's back. Jean bowed and grinned; her dark eyes glared at the large man as he took her hand and kissed it in a similar motion.

"Thank you," Mia said with her bow. Her hesitation and broken accent echoed in Mason's ear. The two women then left them, standing in the walkway, and returned home.

Mason had a lost expression as he watched the woman and did not speak until they were in the house. "You are an odd man, Logan Ezekiel. If I had been Julian, I don't think a gun to my head would have stopped me from pulling the trigger."

"I have no doubt I would have had to fire," Logan stated as he buttoned his jacket, closing the gun away. "But you are not Julian, are you?" The two men turned and quickly embraced each other with a hug.

"It is good to see you," Mason said with a smile.

The meal took most of the day to prepare, and it took a little over thirty minutes for the group to tear into it and finish the meal. Logan stood leaning against the post with the cigar in hand, his sleeves rolled up even in the brisk chilly air. They were expecting more snow, and the long willow tree hung with ice sickles from its limbs.

Mia sat side by side with Jean, a knitting needle I handed when Mason and the two guards stepped out onto the porch to join them. The youngest of the Flannery brothers, Sawyer, walked to the opposite end of the porch past the two women. Passing a glance and smile to Jean as he walked by, he wore a simple white shirt and brown pants held high by suspenders. He wore no gun belt, but Logan did notice the revolver tucked into the back of his pants.

Thomas Flannery walked in the opposite direction, in an almost identical setup, and like his younger brother, neither stopped until they reached the rail on the edge of the porch.

Mason took a seat on the steps beside Logan, "I still can't believe you married her." He gave a passing glance over his shoulder to Mia and Jean, and they both looked at him. Logan continued to look forward as he puffed on the cigar.

Jean stood, and Mia followed suit. "Please don't leave, love." Logan turned and smiled as their eyes connected. She, too, smiled. "It is something you and everyone else will have to accept." He tossed the butt of the cigar out into the thick snow. He walked to Mia, who was still standing, and kissed her. Their foreheads collapsed in on one another as they stared at each other in the eyes.

Logan splashed water on his face, cold and harsh as it tried to freeze his face upon contact. On his knees, he sat in front of the troth so often used to water the horses. He stood and turned; he started to pull the suspenders back over his shirt when he saw her. "Logan Ezekiel." The woman stood in the doorway. Her dress was large and had a plunging neckline. But the most noticeable thing about her was the long flowing blonde hair.

"Viva, can I help you," Logan questioned. He snapped the suspenders back into place, watching the woman.

"The little…" She shook her hand and looked away as if she were looking for a polite word. "Servant girl told me you were here and alone. I thought it would be an enjoyable time for the two of us to get to know one another." The woman grinned without showing any teeth. It was a grin that sent chills down the man's back. He had seen similar smiles from women in the streets of London late at night when he knew what their profession was.

"Where is everyone else?" Logan asked as he ran a hand through his hair and watched as the woman shut the door to the stall they were in.

"Back at the house, enjoying some tea, I believe," she said as she approached the horse in the room with them. It was shut behind a small gate. The old gray horse lowered its head, and she ran her hand down its long nose. "Beautiful creatures, don't you think?" she said as she glanced at Logan, who had not moved. "Do I scare you?"

"No," he replied. He watched her as she stepped away from the horse. She strolled toward him the entire time she was untying the strings holding the dress together at her cleavage.

"I am glad," she stated, looking down at her breasts as she finished the last perfect knot. Slowly, she pulled the dress down her shoulder one by one until it fell free of her body. Logan's eyes grew larger, and his lips parted. The woman stood before him naked. She held her arms out, showing her curvy body, large breasts, thin waist, and big hips. "Do you like?" She smiled as she stepped free of the dress now laid in the hay at her ankles.

"I am married," Logan stated.

"Not what I asked," she said. Now only a step away, she reached, taking his still-damp hands and pulling them to her breasts. They were cool, and he saw her hesitate after the first touch. Then she pulled him closer as her nipples grew harder with his touch. "Do you like?" She stepped toward him, faces close enough as she turned and reached to kiss, but he pulled

away. "I know you like what you see," she stated as she grabbed his crotch.

"I said I am married." He pulled his hands away from her.

"To the little savage, I know," she stated with the same smile as before. "You can keep her. I don't mind sharing if I can call you mine. I wouldn't even be opposed to a little show if it pleases you."

Logan hesitated. Still, he could not stop but look at her body as he stepped toward her. Close enough to touch, he leaned and whispered into her ear. "I am not interested." He walked past her, opened the door, and left her there naked and alone.

Logan stood at the end of the bed, the fire in the room casting dancing shadows across the walls. The bed, big enough for four, turned down and waited with thick covers and large pillows. Mia entered the room in the slip of a gown.

"I am sorry," Logan said immediately when she shut the door. "I thought they would be more accepting."

"I am the one who is sorry," she muttered as she approached another slow kiss.

Logan pulled his arm from behind his back, and in his palm was a small wooden box. "What is this?"

"I accept you for who you are." He opened it to expose the small white feather. "Little feather!"

Chapter Twelve

They had spent most of the evening going through the town, finding next to nothing that would be helpful, and they returned to the Ulysses. Mia hung to the back of the group, and she could see the ship long before they broke through the tree line to where the airship had landed. When they reached the clearing, the doors were shut, and once they were close enough, a horn sounded somewhere in the ship. The sound of chains getting caught in metal echoed through the foggy bottom. It continued what seemed like forever until it was firmly rested on the ground in front of them.

Mia sighed. She had dreaded coming back to the ship and facing all the problems she'd been away from for less than a day. He stood with his arms crossed against his chest, and his face was red with anger, making her dread the short walk up the ramp even more. Mia handed the reigns of the horse off to a waiting Frost and couldn't help herself as she looked down on the man.

"Was expecting Julian to greet us," Hardy said, taking as he did the same as his companion.

"You need to come with us," William Beck said from the opposite doorway. He had a similar disposition as Frost. He couldn't hide his anger.

Mia's heart stopped. William's normally cheerful expression was gone, replaced with a hollow dread. "What happened?" she quickly asked. Her first thought was of Sophia.

Kent, also right behind her, could not hide his worry. They followed Beck up two levels until they came to Julian's room. Upon entering the room, the smell was enough to cause them to pause. "He took the fever late in the night," Beck said, letting the two of them walk into the room. Both held hands over their faces. "We were hoping to get to a doctor in town."

"The town is abandoned," Hardy stated. Beck ran a hand over his bald head, and the voice cut through the air.

"As… planned…" It was Julian, but the voice was that of an old wheezing man.

"He has been insisting we keep to our schedule as best we can," Beck stated, stepping outside the room, Mia glared at him.

"Where is Sophia?" she questioned.

"Safely in her room."

Mia rushed past him, down the small hall, and up the stairs. She seemed not to even breathe through the brisk run until she came to the door to Sophia's room. She hesitated only for a moment before she stepped in. The girl sat on her bed with a book in hand. With a breath of relief, the girl was still alive.

Sophia smiled when she saw her, lifted her hand to her face, and ran her fingers from her forehead down to her cheek. Mia placed her hand on her cheek and immediately realized the young girl saw the scratches on her face. "An accident, but I am okay. Are you okay?" The girl nodded. "Are you enjoying your book?" Mia shut the door behind her. She took another deep breath.

"Sophia…" there was a hesitation as she approached the bed and sat on the edge. The little girl shut her book, keeping a finger on her desired page. "Has anyone been bothering you?"

Sophia shook her head now. Mia felt guilty and stupid. With her and Hardy off the ship, it would have been easy for someone to have taken Sophia.

"If someone was bothering you, or if you had a secret, would you try to tell me?" Mia questioned.

There was a distinct hesitation in Sophia's response as she glanced off to the side and then back to Mia. She slowly shook her head yes.

"You do have a secret?" Mia questioned.

The hesitation was still there before the little girl shook her head. She was lying. Her ward knew something, something she was not willing to tell her. There were already too many questions and secrets in Mia's life, and to learn Sophia had one as well caused an obvious expression of worry.

Hardy knocked on the open door thrice. "Beck wants to see you."

"Why me?" Mia quickly questioned as she stood from the bed, giving Sophia one last look.

"He is asking to speak to everyone," Hardy said. "I will stay with Sophia until you are back." Sophia smiled when he spoke, and Mia noticed the look between them. Mia realized whatever secret Sophia kept had to do with Hardy.

"I will be back," she stated, getting up and leaving the room.

• • •

Mia walked into the engineer's room, the same room she had found Sophia in before. But she found William Beck in a much more unique way this trip than the one before. Goggles on his forehead, he leaned over with arms spread wide on the table, glaring at the paper in front of him. "Two days," he said, pointing to the map. "Two days Northwest of here is a small trading outpost. We are going to set down right on the edge of town. Risk the spectacle of it all. There will be a doctor there. There is an army fort there. But there must be a doctor there that can help Julian."

He never looked at Mia; he just continued to glare at the map. "It is not what he wants," she replied, walking across the room and taking a glance at the map. "He wants us to continue."

"It is the same, Mia, the same symptoms as the fever my father had. Is the same rash-like redness, the same wheeze, the same hysterical dreams I was told my father had." He stood, crossing his arms across his chest. "Julian Bastion has been poisoned by someone on the Ulysses. The same poison used to kill my father. It is a chance to get him some help and get him through this. Maybe he can tell me who here has cause for seeing him dead…" He glared at Mia accusingly.

"We have yet to take off. Is there a reason why…" Mia questioned, still standing in the doorway. The storms had passed, but the Ulysses was still grounded.

"I am assuming command of the Ulysses until further notice," Beck said sternly. Mia felt his presence before his touch, the twist of her arm at her side pulling out into the hall and pushing into the opposite wall.

"I should just kill you now," Frost's voice echoed in her ear. "Be done with all this trouble, but Mister Beck is too cautious. He wants to know the guilty party before we hang you from the rafters in the cargo hold."

"I wasn't on the ship," she muttered. She felt his hand rip at the vest until the buttons were gone and then ripped harder until the axe came free and clanked harshly on the floor at her feet.

"It could have been a slow reaction, ingested days before he fell ill... you two had a private meeting days ago, one you initiated..." Beck said from the other room he would not even look in the direction of what was happening. She knew the blade was there before the harsh sound of her dress being cut downward. With the touch of his cold hand on her inner thigh, then on the outside of her leg, he ripped the single pistol from the garter, leaving scratches with his nails.

She could feel Frost's breath on her ear and neck; he kept her pinned to the wall with his right arm. "Any other weapons," he hissed.

"Frost... no harm is to come to come to her until we get to the bottom of all of this," he glared back at the other man.

"Fine," he yelped back, pulling her away from the wall, his left hand now with a handful of hair, "Going to lock her away with the others."

• • •

Mia sat looking at the locked door in front of her. She did not even know these rooms were there. The third level of the Ulysses and these rooms were meant for one purpose. To hold people prisoner, long steel bars with reinforced doors meant to keep the largest of men from breaking free. She had finished tearing the dress just below the knee, and now she sat on the excess. The back of the dress was still split from Frost's knife, and the floor under her was rigid and hard. The rooms must have been directly over the steam engines. The walls seemed to sweat constantly, adding to the indescribable smell. Her skin pooled to the touch of dirt and sweat. She had not eaten in days, and now the only thing on her mind was Julian Bastion.

Mia knew she did not poison the man; the guilty party was still somewhere on board. Walking free and ready to kill. It had also crept into her mind; this may have nothing to do with Sophia. She heard him cough so many times over the hours. She was unsure how much time had passed since Frost pushed her into the cell and locked the door behind her. But it was at least twenty times the sound of his cough that echoed through the cell across from her, the sound of a war drum.

Mia did not call out his name; she had not seen him since he left her room the evening after the fight with Frost. Gareth was also a prisoner, leaving several other questions. If Gareth was so connected with the Bastion family, why was he now locked away like her? Her head lay against the hard wall. There were too many questions, and nothing was being answered. Where was her husband, Logan Ezekiel? Who was responsible for the death of Stephen Beck? Who wanted a little girl dead? Who was the assassin? Was this the same person responsible for the poisoning of Julian Bastion? How did Hardy know about the name Little Feather? What was Sophia's secret? But the one question that kept resurfacing was, why her?

Mia's skin crawled with anticipation and anger. She kept thinking about the old man and how he left her no choice. And now, what would she do if she could get her firsthand Frost or William Beck? Hardy had said she was more dangerous than anyone else could imagine. As she gritted her teeth and ran her tongue against the roof of her mouth, all she could taste was blood.

• • •

Mia heard his heavy steps come down the hall. Thin boots under heavy bodies on solid wood left a dance running through her mind. She stood and quickly approached the door. Smith peaked into the room; a puff of air escaped him reminiscent of an old bull exhaling as he glared into the dark. The clank and cling of the metal plate against the slot low on the door as he pushed the plate into the openness. The moment flesh was exposed, she kicked. The sound of the bone being broken echoed through the room. Quickly, she went back into the corner, glaring at the scattered food on her floor. The man yelled out in pain, no understandable words; she smiled. Bloodshot eyes glared at the door, tears of anger about to escape. Mia waited. He had to come in now, and she was ready.

Nothing. The door never opened. She only heard him rush from the hall, still mumbling and cussing out. She knew she had broken at least his wrist. This would bring Beck to her. Or Frost… let it be Frost. She was ready for him. This was her choice, and she had made it.

• • •

Mia sat in the corner, watching the food. The growling of her stomach startled her each time it sang. At least an hour had passed since Smith ran from the hall, but no one had come. "That is the first bit of food I have seen in a day," she heard Gareth mutter. She stood and slowly approached the door and small window out into the hall. In the dim light and dark cell, the only thing she could see of him was his hands. Those massive hands she could still remember tearing at her clothing. She wanted them, but repressed it. His face appeared from the shadows with a crooked half-smile. Once again, it reminded her of Logan. "Why now? "I think you broke his hand; I heard the pop like a musket even over here," their eyes now locked onto each other.

"His wrist, I know I did," she replied, fighting back the smile. He did not as Gareth laughed a thunderous sound in the echoed hallow hall.

"Is Julian dead?" Gareth questioned; his eyes glared to the floor.

"He was still alive before… before this," she too looked again at her empty cell.

The jarring feel of the Ulysses moving almost knocked her from her feet. If not for her hands resting inside of the bars, she would have fallen to the floor. The steam engulfed the room, and she began to cough, and her eyes watered. Her heart raced; they had been sitting for hours wondering why they were just taking off now.

Her bare feet sloshed through the food on the floor, making it slicker to stand. "Gareth," she questioned with a pause. His head leaned against the door until she spoke.

"Yes, Mia?" he looked almost calm from across the hall.

"Could you have killed Frost the day on the viewing deck?" she questioned.

"Julian asked me to break him, not kill him. He wanted information. He never said about what," Gareth questioned. "The only reason I didn't break him or throw him over the edge at the start of the fight." Mia smiled, but in her stomach, she was glad of one thing. Julian never told Gareth why he wanted Frost broken and vulnerable. Frost had to be the one sent to kill Sophia. Now, she was locked away in a cell with only Hardy between him and his assignment. But she knew Hardy would not be taken as unaware as she was.

"What about Owens?"

"I'm here," the kid called out from another cell, his voice more cracked than she could ever remember it.

• • •

Mia didn't remember lying down in the corner of the cell. She lay with the bottom of her dress she had torn as a pillow. The sound of a ring clicking against the bars woke her. She looked up to see Beck there, staring into the room.

"You are only making things more difficult. You should eat," he stated. Mia looked and saw the fresh plate of food at the door. "We will be at the fort in a day; Julian still fights and may pull through it." Mia sat up, wondering if she had been in the cell for a day and a half already.

"You know I didn't do it," Mia whispered, pushing her way off the floor and to her feet. As she got closer, Beck pulled away from the bars, and she smiled.

"Right now, Frost and Smith would like nothing more than to come in here, hang you from the ceiling, and call it a day," Beck stated. He was now in the center of the hall. As Mia approached, she could see Gareth's hands still there, extended out of the bars.

"He can stir a pot with one good hand," Gareth stated. Beck smiled and glanced back at the bigger man. It was unfathomable what would happen now if the bigger man were free from his cell. There was intense anger in Gareth's eyes. Mia knew the look well; she had no doubt she shared it. "And Frost can come to pay me a visit any time," Gareth added, Beck again focusing his look on Mia.

"I am sorry about this. I am. I promise no harm will come to you… either of you." He looked down the hall, no doubt glancing at Owens. His hands were now crossed behind his back. "I told one person about the letter from my father. The poison... that was you, Mia. No one else knew about it."

"No one except the person who poisoned your father." She glared into his eyes, his face twisted away. "Daniel Hope was suspected of poisoning your father. What if it was not Sophia's father but someone else? Someone here on this ship with us right under you."

"It is all possible, but why? Why poison the captain and not me?" Beck replied.

"Maybe the target was you," Mia stated. Beck smiled; the thought had crossed his mind. "Let me out of here. Let me see Julian."

"As I said, he still lives. Hardy is looking out for Sophia. You will be released soon enough," Beck turned, walking down the hall. Mia held her breath until she heard the large door at the end of the hall shut.

"You have a plan?" Gareth questioned, taking a tight grip on the bar, and began to pull and jerk harshly against them.

"At the moment, no… we just can't be here when they get to the fort," Mia stated.

"Be a little hard to escape. I mean, if we get out of here, there is still the little fact we are airborne," Gareth said with a smile. She wished he would stop smiling at her because each time he did so, she could feel her pulse quicken and her legs grow weak.

Chapter Thirteen

The door crept open, and the soft rumble of boots walking through the hall forced Mia to her feet. "If you try anything, I will shoot you." Frost's voice sent a chill down her back. The sound of the hammer on the pistol being pulled back forced her to step closer to the door. It would be harder for him to shoot her. He would have to stick his entire arm in to get a shot, and she could attack.

The keys made an eerie sound in the hollow room. A moment of dread overtook her as the door crept open. "Out, now," he barked his orders. Mia didn't move. "Now, damn it." Mia moved closer to the door.

"Where are we going?" Mia questioned.

"Julian is awake…" He motioned with his gun for her to step out. Mia walked out in front of him, keeping her hands at her sides. "If I wanted you dead, I would just shoot you now, savage. The captain wants to see you."

Julian lay on the bed with his arms clasped across his chest, but unlike before, his head moved when the door opened. The bronzed mask sitting at the bedside table left a distorted image of the room as she walked in. Beside the mask rested her small axe, her derringer pistol, and the revolver still with its belt and holster. She took a moment to cautiously look over her shoulder. Frost did not enter the room. Like a scolded dog, he was in Julian's eyesight but moved no closer. "Please sit," he mumbled, shifting his legs off the bed. His hand shook uncontrollably. He tried to stabilize it with his other unsuccessfully.

"Help me sit up." Mia took his arms, pulling him up into a sitting position in his bed. Julian smiled, turning away from a violent cough. Blood leaked from the corner of his mouth as he tried to clear it with a piece of stained cloth. "I kind of thought I would die fighting, not laying on my back."

"You're not dying," she quickly replied. She didn't know if he would live or not. It just felt like the right thing to say.

"We both know I am," Julian stated. "How is Sophia?"

"With Hardy," she replied.

"Do you trust him?" he questioned, twisting his head to look at her. He shook as if he was freezing, but the room was suffocating hot.

"I do," she answered.

"They think you poisoned me… I have set Beck on the proper path. He will not lock you back up," he stated.

"You told him about Sophia and the threat?" she questioned. It crept into her mind again. Beck was the threat. Only two people on the vessel she was sure were no threat to the little girl—Julian and Hardy. Even Gareth, to whom she had a connection, was a lustful attraction she could not rule out.

"I told him enough, but not everything, enough to make him agree to let you free," Julian stated. Like a hollow tree in a windstorm, he fell over and rolled back onto the bed.

"And Gareth?" Mia questioned.

"Should be released any moment. Gareth is a loyal subservient of my brother… he would only act in such a deceitful way if ordered by Hamilton," Julian stated. "I do not see a reason for my brother to want me gone from this life. I need my rest; I will send for you again shortly."

"Owens?"

Julian grumbled. "I still don't know what to do with the journalist…"

"Leave him locked up," Mia replied. She trusted the writer, but he was too unknown to her. Of all the men on the vessel, he served no purpose to the ship or Sophia. "It was best he stays locked up at least a while longer."

Mia retrieved her weapons, leaving the room, giving him one last glance before exiting. She stepped out expecting to see Frost, but no one waited for her. She would check in on Sophia before she did anything else.

The moment she entered the room, she lifted her hands to show she was armed. Hardy sat with his pistol aimed at her, and it seemed to last forever before he lowered it. His hat sat on the bed in front of Sophia, whose nose was buried in a book. Mia smiled as their eyes met. "How is she doing?"

"Better now, I am sure," Hardy stated.

"Do you mind watching over her a while longer?" Mia questioned, watching the man lean back in his chair. His posture told her he didn't. The gun rested on his lap. She was better here with him than her, anyways.

• • •

Mia had started to undress the moment she entered her room. The torn vest first, though she wasn't sure when she had ripped the buttons from this one. The lower part of the dress, what was left of it, slid free shortly after entering the wash area of the quarters, the steel pan filled with ice-cold water. She quickly splashed it across her face. She untied the corset and let it fall where she stood like everything else. Only a moment to shimmy the loose white pants, torn off at the knees much like the dress, the loose laced white shirt. Mia stood staring at her naked reflection; dark circles made her eyes look darker than usual. Mia walked to the opposite side of the room, pulling the axe from the ruined vest. Mia lifted the blade to her hair and began to pull it against the sharp edge. Lots of dirty black hair littered the floor at her feet. She never stopped until her once shoulder-length straight-cut hair was chopped and uneven, cut with long strands reaching the bottom of her ears.

Mia splashed chilly water on her face and knocked loose hair from her bare shoulders and skin. Her mouth twitched as she stared at the reflection.

Mia rushed across the room, lifting the suitcase, and quickly unlatched it, pulling a black slip out and then over her head. She pulled the red and black corset and began to latch it around her, pushing her breasts up in the suffocating leather. She pulled the black stockings out as she sat on the bed and up over her feet, stretching close to the thighs. Then came the dress. She latched it around her, avoiding adding the hoop under. She returned to the mirror, splashed the oil into her hands, and started to push her hair upward off the side of her head. She smiled as she cleaned her hands of the oil. She opened the small containers, two of them red and black. Slowly, she ran the black over and under her eyes across her face, leaving no flesh to be seen for a full inch across above and below her eyes. Again, she cleaned her hands, then the blood-red color, two stripes on each cheek running down toward her jaw. She picked the axe up from the small table, and before she turned, Kent Hardy stood leaning against the door.

"Been there long?" she questioned, stepping out of the small wash area and looking at Hardy. She had not asked before but could see the sling on the arm where he had been shot.

"Long enough," he replied, "you look like someone with ill intentions."

Mia crossed the room, putting the axe on the bed, and picked up the suitcase, the last vest she had brought on the trip. One was ruined by Gareth in a moment of lust, the other by Frost in anger. But this one was special to her. She put her arms through the holes and began to button it, a couple of sizes too big for her frame. This solid black vest with only a couple of white stitches out of place on the pockets came from the most respected tailors across the sea. This was Logan's vest. She buttoned it close without putting the axe inside; she picked the necklace with the small white feather from the bed and put it around her neck. "I guess there is no way I can tell you from doing something stupid, is there?"

"Just watch Sophia for me," Mia stated, walking out into the hall past him with a white-knuckled grip on the axe.

• • •

There was no hesitation in Mia's movement entering the engineer's room. She saw her target. Beck's arms crossed with only a passing glance back. "You did not have the balls to even come to release me yourself?" she started crossing the room, taking up a defensive stance a few paces from him. She could have just killed him on entry, but she wanted answers.

"If you are seeking an apology, you won't get one," Beck stated, messing with the hair on his chin. "I did what I thought was right at the time. As acting captain, I had every right to suspect you and lock you away."

Stone entered the room, pausing at the door. The two looked at him. "Is it done?" Beck questioned.

"Yes," Stone stated.

"Is what done," Mia quickly asked, keeping an eye on both men the best she could. She remembered Beck telling her how close Stone was to his father.

"We found this," Beck pulled his free hand away from his body, opening to show a small pale gray powder contained in an opened leather pouch. "We believe it is what was used to poison the captain."

She quickly asked.

"Smith… he was trying to put it in your food after you broke his wrist," Stone stated.

"He confessed… we will keep him locked away until we get to California," Beck stated.

"And your father?" Mia questioned.

"He also confessed to poisoning my father," Beck answered. "I reported to Julian in an attempt to get him to let us land… possibly get him help."

"And he insists on continuing as planned," Mia stated. Her nerves had calmed, and the adrenaline wore off, causing her hand to tremble. "Can I speak to Smith?"

Beck gave her an odd glance before looking back out the windows of the Ulysses. "You may talk to him, but he stays locked away. He will stand trial for the murder of two good men."

She stopped at the door and looked back at Beck. "When did you realize it was him?"

"The food I brought you was prepared by me… I had hoped to make it a peace offering before I let you and Gareth free." Mia could see the somber look on his face reflected in the glass.

Mia found humor in the fact Smith was in the very prison cell she had been locked away in a couple of hours earlier. The same cell she used to break his hand. She gleamed into the room, seeing his massive frame sitting in the back corner. He laughed when their eyes met. "What do you want?" he questioned, with his bull frog ugly expression. His distorted face always looked angry, with thick lips and nearly no eyebrows.

"Simple, I want to know why?" she questioned.

He laughed. It was a laugh of a man who knew more than he would ever say. "What do you want to know?" he questioned. "Why I foolishly let a frail of a squaw anger me and get me discovered. I was foolish. All I had to do was wait, but I wanted you dead."

"And Sophia?" she questioned.

He twisted his head to one side in confusion, an honest look of unknowing. Another she could mark off the list. "Why would I want to kill the girl?"

Mia looked at a nearby cell. She could see Owens's arms reached out. "Why Julian?"

The man smiled as he stood, careful not to touch his broken hand on anything as he crept toward the door. "The head of the serpent," he stated. "Cut the head, and the body will wither and die."

Mia paused. "You wanted to bring the ship down?"

"I thought it would make it easier for me to slip into the control room and crash this godless creation," he stated, lifting his hand for a moment. "But still, someone always remained right there at the controls. I would have to poison another, even two, and my time was running out."

Mia asked nothing else; she didn't need to know anything else. She left him standing there and walked away. The suspect list was down to four, Frost, Stone, Beck, or Gareth. One of those four wanted Sophia dead, but why? As she started up the steps, the only thing she could think was *let it be Frost.*

Mia stopped to check on Julian. The man still breathed. She glanced at the bucket at his side. He had been spitting up a lot of blood. It would not be long now. She stood at his bedside, his eyes closed, and his chest slowly rose and fell with each breath. The man would live another day, two at the most. She placed her hand on his head for just a second, a moment of respect for a man she once hated. A man who hated her. Mia was exhausted, and though some things had cleared up, questions still needed to be answered. But all she wanted to do was sleep.

• • •

Exhausted and hungry, her hand trembling as she touched the doorknob of her room. Mia let her forehead rest on the exterior in her hesitation. Her skin felt odd. The sweat pooled against the door for a moment before pulling away. Like her hand, she stepped away from the door and walked to the end of the hall. Nineteen steps up what felt like forever before reaching the door to the outside. The air chilled the sweat the moment it cracked into the night; Mia moved the distance to the railing on instinct till she rested against the iron barrier.

The sound of the hammer being pulled back into place was as loud as any crack of thunder. Mia closed her eyes as she turned slowly to face Frost. Frost stood, gun in hand, aimed directly at her. A confused expression on his face. He was pale. He had been waiting there for her. "Just going to shoot me?" she questioned. She tightly gripped the axe.

"It would be the smart way, wouldn't it?" he questioned, the gun held high. She could see his eye looking at her down the short barrel. "One shot, right through the heart after everything. I think people would believe me if I told them you attacked me and I was only defending myself. Throw your body over the edge. It would be so easy."

"Then why don't you do it," her hand twitched. One sign of her lifting the axe and it would give him his reason to fire.

The man smiled, looking to the floor in front of him, and released the hammer back into a safe position. He raised the pistol, pointing the muzzle toward the canvas above. "Coward's way," he stated, tossing the gun to the floor. Mia took a step forward, and he smiled as he started to undo the buttons on his shirt. He pulled it free from his pants when he was done and tossed it to the floor. He reached behind his back, pulling the knife from its sheath. Mia knew only one of them was leaving the observation deck alive.

Frost twirled the long blade in his hand. This was not the same knife he had been using. This blade was longer, reaching at least six inches and thick, made for cutting into flesh. He circled away from her. Mia let the handle of the axe slip till she felt the blade close to her grip. She was not going to attack; she'd let the much bigger and stronger man come to her. Frost came, pushing the blade in the direction of her stomach. Twice, he thrust, and twice, Mia avoided his attack. Frost grumbled, standing straight. This was what he wanted, but he did not expect her to hesitate. His face was covered in frustration. He wanted to cut her, even kill her. He flipped the knife over, holding the blade downward and out. He did not charge her now. He crept, sliding his feet from one side to the other, backing her away from the edge. There would be no jabs this time. He wanted to corner her; he continued to shift and slide with each step she took, a similar one backward. He leaped.

Mia rolled under him, turning as she came to her feet, bringing the axe upward in a quick motion, cutting deep into his back. Three quick steps back away from him. He swung violently with the knife while the other hand grabbed at the open wound. Frost rushed her, swinging his knife wildly, easy for her to dodge. Mia ran the axe across his abdomen, cutting another deep gash into his flesh. She turned again as he stood inspecting the wound on his side, exposed muscle and flesh. He looked over his shoulder at her. Both cuts bled rapidly. They were survivable wounds if he got help soon, but if he didn't, if he continued to pursue her, all she would have to do was avoid him until he was too weak.

The man bit his lip as he turned, facing Mia. He switched his knife to his off-hand, leaning down and pulling a second blade from his boot. It was the small knife he had used on her before. Mia said nothing, pacing away from him. She stopped moving once he was again in a standing position. "I am going to enjoy this. I only wish I could have some more fun with you first," Frost walked forward. He was showing no effects from the wounds, though now his pants were soaked with his blood.

Closer and closer, Frost stalked, and then she saw it, the weave. He leaned in the direction of the wound on his left abdomen. Her grip was tight, and she had a spot of attack. He leaped again, but this time, he did the unexpected. The knife fell to the floor in front of her as his left hand grabbed at the back of the dress and pulled her backward. Harshly, her head bounced off the floor, and he was on top of her, the blade to her cheek. Wide-eyed, pinning her with his knees across her arms, the short knife touched her face but did not cut. He ran his free hand across his side, looking at the bright blood; she knew he would be more worried if the blood was dark. He looked down, their eyes met, and he smiled again.

Frost's blood-soaked hand on her throat, he took a glance at the pinned axe as he began to squeeze her throat. The knife rested on his leg; he released his hold when she began to struggle for oxygen. "Maybe I can have some fun after all," he said, placing the blade of the knife on her forehead at the bottom of her scalp. "How is it you savages do that, cut just deep enough to rip the flesh from a man's head? I never quite understood the purpose of such an assault. Wasn't the embarrassment of being killed by a lesser enough for you? You had to go and maim a man."

Mia gritted her teeth. She tried to push him, but his weight was too much for her. "Such a pretty face to cut up," he stated, pulling the blade back to her cheek and running it across the left side of her face, this time cutting until he saw blood. "I understand the appeal, like taking a wolf for a pet. Fucking a savage. Did you dominate Logan Ezekiel in the bedroom? Did he let the animal out?" She again pushed against his weight, but nothing. She was at his mercy.

"You will never know," she spat in his face. He smiled as he wiped his forehead clean.

"You think I would want to touch you?" he said, placing the blade to her throat. She saw nothing but hatred in the man's eyes. "Irony, kill you with your weapon." He reached with his free hand for the axe in her grip.

As he struggled to pull it free, his right leg unpinned her arm. Something he never saw coming. When he had dropped the larger of the two knives, she had picked it up when he jerked her back to the floor. The large blade dug deep into the soft between his chest and shoulder. She pulled down forcefully, shredding through muscle, flesh, and tendons. The man rolled away in pain. To the floor, he scurried away from her on his one good arm. He came to a stop, resting on his knees, pulling the knife free. He had no use for his right arm. Frost turned, favoring his shoulder. He picked the knife up with his only good arm.

Mia, still on her hands and knees, looked up at him. He glanced at his arm. If he did live through this, he was certain he would lose it. He twisted his neck and looked at her. "You will pay for that."

Mia stood, axe in one hand, using the other to wipe the blood clear from her face. It mixed with the war pain already there, covering her cheek in red. She smiled. He had size and strength before, but now, without the use of one arm, the fight was close to even. Frost stalked forward. As he thrust the knife forward, she went to his weaker side. The cut across his side and a dead arm she cut deep into his ribs above the previous cut.

Frost stopped at the rail. He used the iron bars to hold him upright. He turned, his lips covered in blood. "You think you beat me?" He smiled.

Mia stood up straight, waiting for him to attack again. He dropped his remaining knife; it bounced off the rail with a clang, disappearing. Frost looked up and around at the Ulysses. "Truly is a marvelous thing." He followed his knife into the darkness below.

Mia rushed to the edge, dropping to her knees, part of her hoping to see him there hanging on. She could see nothing but the bleak shadows of the surface passing below. She turned with her back to the railing, shutting her eyes. She took a deep breath. If what she believed was true, the man who was on the vessel to kill the little girl was now dead. She smiled, and even a hint of laughter escaped her. She would have to tell Julian and Beck. She laughed, crawling to her knees and then to a standing position.

• • •

Mia found Beck sitting at the controls to Ulysses. He turned when she entered and showed no reaction to the blood smeared across her face. "Frost?" he questioned; the goggles covered his eyes, but she saw only blankness from the rest of his face.

"Dead," she stated. Her axe was safely hidden in her vest. A vest still in one piece, something she was thankful for.

"Too bad there will be many questions I'll have to answer when I return to Washington. The elder Frost will not be too happy," he said. There was a slight grin across his face. "He was intelligent, more than just a simple soldier, did you know that? These goggles were his ideas, not mine."

"It was either him or me," she stated.

"I am sure you believe that, but when you came here earlier, you would have killed me if given half the thought I meant you harm," Beck said. She didn't consider Beck a threat, but as he twisted and looked back at her with his arms crossed against his chest, his forearms exposed due to his rolled-up sleeves. William Beck was much larger than she remembered. She stepped back on her left leg, her strongest, and if she had to move from some sort of attack, she wasn't entirely sure she could even get off another attack from anyone.

"I believe that he intended me harm from the moment I got on this blasted ship, and I don't appreciate your tone…"

Beck uncrossed your arms and looked away from her for a moment, and she clenched her jaw. "I don't intend to offend you or put you off in any way."

"I did not come on this ship looking for violence…"

"It is exactly what you came here looking for, and it is understandable with the absence of your husband, and…" Again, Beck paused as he glared out the visage window of the Ulysses. "I considered Frost a friend and, in some ways, a comparable mind in the evolution of this ship…"

"I'm sorry for your friend," Mia tried to stand up straight, but she ached all over.

Beck looked back at her for a moment and pushed his goggles up on his forehead. "I know you didn't want to kill him, and he backed you into a corner. Forgive my words, Mia Ezekiel."

Mia watched as his expression seemed to go over his thoughts; his expression changed a lot from one moment to the other, and he looked through her. "What is it?" Mia questioned.

Beck ran a hand through his beard. "Maybe you should go get yourself cleaned up."

"Is Julian awake?" she questioned.

"He was sleeping peacefully the last I saw him," he replied.

"Very well, Captain Beck."

Chapter Fourteen

Mia sat in silence with her head leaning back on the edge of the ceramic clawfoot tub. She felt the ship lean to one side, and she opened her eyes, looking up at the rafters. She thought they were oak, but they were painted black, hiding most of the wood. The ceiling was littered with copper piping running all throughout, much similar to the piping that was coming to the bathtub she had found herself. The heated water engulfed her entire body, leaving just her neck above the glassy surface. She had come to enjoy the sensation of a warm bath while living as Logan's wife. This was the closest she had felt to being comfortable since Ulysses took flight. Only after she visited Julian, who was peacefully sleeping, did she make the journey back to the third level. The same level as the prison cells. She had not known about the cells before, but she knew they were necessary. The vibrations of the moving ship were made noticeable by the ripples in the water. Her head leaned against the hard edge of the tub once again, trying to remember the bath back home in Boston, but each time she closed her eyes, she pictured Gareth sending a feeling of warmth through her already heated body.

Mia sat up, trying to flush the image of the shirtless brute from her mind. She used the soft, warm washcloth to clean the wound on her face from Frost's blade. With each touch, it stung, but she was alive, even though the odds were against her. She had a cut on her lower lip. She did not know how, but she suspected she bit her lip sometime during the fight. Mia felt the start of a headache from having been thrown to the floor by the man, several other scratches, bruises, and random aches. The bath cured it all, at least for now, and in her mind, it was a cure-all. She couldn't help but think about each strike she laid into the man. She snorted an uncomfortable laugh. There was no point in pondering on something she could not change. If by some miraculous chance Frost was alive, he was now dozens of miles behind them.

Mia moved her arms to the tub's edge, dropping her head under the water. Mia held her breath for as long as she could, staring up through the water. She rose, black strands of unevenly chopped hair littering her face as she spat water from her mouth in a steady stream until it was only a sputter. She sat up, pushing the hair from her eyes, still feeling the rush.

She smiled. It wasn't from happiness or anything of the sort. It was uneasy as she felt the rush she'd gotten so often from previous fights in her life. Her hand shook, she was coming down, and her pulse had returned to normal from the fight. The feeling was different; she knew she had killed the man, but the hatred for him made her fingers itch. It wasn't enough. She had not killed him. Not really. He fell to his death before she could finish him, no matter the silliness of what Beck had planted in her thoughts. This was different from the old man in town; the hatred made it different: a kill with a purpose behind it instead of senseless violence.

Mia again slid down the tub under the water, using her hands on the edge of the tub to hold her under the steaming surface. The thought was still there, like a growling within her stomach for food. What if Frost was not the assassin? Could she be so sure of her motivations to have the young man dead, or was it pure hatred? A genuine hatred over having the soldier assault her not once but twice. The second time, she could not retaliate. Thrown into a cell to rot over something she had not done. Beck had said as much. She had come looking for violence. Using the excuse of Frost being the assassin was just that, an excuse for her rage.

"Shit," she gargled, letting the water escape from her lungs under the water. If there had been anyone watching, they may have even thought she was trying to drown herself. But she felt regret now, repentance of possibly killing a man who didn't have to die.

Mia slowly came back to the surface. Only her mouth, nose, and part of her face came up for air. A deep breath later, she again submerged under the cooling water. The sting of heat was gone now. Or maybe it was the adrenaline finally leaving her body that made the water seem frigid. She came up for air in a rush as she sat flat in the tub, her shoulders and head above the water. She stood, though Ulysses was always so hot. Now, her skin took a chill as her wet body felt the touch of air. There was a plug in the bottom, leading to a drain outside the Ulysses. She stepped out of the tub, and there was a mirror on the opposite wall of the small room. She approached, glaring at the cut in the mirror. Slowly, she touched and flinched the moment her fingers hit flesh. The cut would no doubt scar. At least the self-inflicted scratches on the same side of her face would not, even if they were still visible.

Mia slipped the boots over bare, wet feet, dragging the white shirt over her head and arms through before she pulled the dress to her hips and secured it in place. A last look at her still red face in the mirror and soaked hair, messy and unpredictable, lay on her forehead and ears. She left the room with a bundle of clothing and an axe in her arms. She walked up the stairs, feeling lighter on her feet. The adrenaline from the fight was gone now. The bath had done all she wanted. She came to the mess hall. Gareth looked at her and didn't smile; he was just sitting with a mostly empty plate before him. He wore a shirt, half a button above his abdomen. "I see you found the bath stations," he smirked. Still, his adoring smile was absent, but she found herself looking past his smile to his set muscular jawline, which seemed chiseled in stone.

Mia crossed the room and took a seat on the opposite side of the table; she said nothing as the two stared at each other. Over a minute passed before he smiled and looked away from her. For only a moment, he looked at the plate and pushed it away. "You cut your hair," he said with a point of his large fingers. "It looks… like you." She smiled in reply, sitting the bundle on the table in front of her. She was still staring at his perfect jawline and the smirk of his lips. "It is good to be out of the holding cells." Gareth leaned over the table and placed a finger on her face just under the cut. "Who did this? Was it Frost?"

"Doesn't matter," she replied with a half-smile as she lowered her head. His hands were callused, but his touch was gentle on her face as she placed a hand on his wrist but did not push it away.

Gareth looked at her hand before he removed his hand, but she still felt his warm touch; the hairs on her arms stood with excitement. He never pulled from her grip, but he stared at her hands as she looked at them on the table between them. His strong, rough hands, with such a gentle touch, were more than twice the size of her own. "It does matter," Gareth pulled away from her grip, and she could see the intensity in his eyes. He stood, but before he could move away from the table, she had a tight grip on his wrist once again. He looked back; he could easily pull away from her. But he waited. She walked around the other end of the table and stopped only a step away, and she could feel the heat coming off his body as his breathing quickened. He turned back to her again, putting his other hand close to her face and placing an outstretched finger on the fresh wound on her face. "It was Frost, wasn't it? I'll break him."

"Frost is dead." She placed a hand on his wrist and, for a moment, let her head rest in his massive palm. Or so she hoped he was, no matter the regret she felt earlier.

"You…" he said in hesitation, breaking her from her daze. He already knew the answer and had begun to smile. Even his breathing had begun to slow. She closed her eyes, feeling his plush through her grip on his wrist. When the moment had passed, she opened her eyes, pulled her head away from his hand slowly, and shook a nodding yes as she glanced up at him.

"I wish I could have seen it." She shook her head, not releasing the grip on his hand, turned to the table and picked up her things.

As Mia turned back, Gareth never moved, only stood there watching her. She gave him a passing smile, stepping closer to the man. He towered over her in every way, his broad shoulders and his height. She felt lost in his shadow. She stepped closer and closer to him until her chin almost rested on his chest as she gleamed up at him with her dark eyes. It was there again, the half-crooked smile she often compared to her husband's. That glance should have been enough to stop her thoughts, to stop her actions from going any further.

Mia felt guilty; it had been so long now since her husband left her to do some unknown foolish tasks for Hamilton Bastion. Something dangerous even though Logan was not a violent man, he had become adequate with a gun. What made Logan so dangerous was his sympathy and intelligence, two things in the world that led him to his death. She had given up hope. Over a year was a long time to hold on to the unknown. Now she stood looking into Gareth's eyes, a man she was uncontrollably attracted to. He was nothing like

Logan. She had no doubt the man was an incredibly dangerous man of unknown intelligence.

Mia knew, in her heart, that Logan was dead. There was nothing in this world that would have kept him away if he'd been otherwise. Could anyone truly blame her? She had to go on and live her life. She found his hand with her free hand, brought it up to her mouth, and slowly kissed the top. The entire time, she kept a look at his eyes, and she saw the moment he realized what was happening. There was no smile or words, only a narrowing of his dark eyes. She turned, beginning to walk away from him. She did not have to look back. She could feel him no more than a step behind as his shadow loomed over her own as they entered the hallway.

As they stepped into the hallway, she was leading him to her room, but she felt his hand take hold of her shoulder and drag her backward. Before she could say anything, they were inside his room, the first door inside the hall on the right. She had not even realized he had a room here, thinking he was housed in the lower part of the Ulysses. The room was dark; she stood at the door as he struck the match bizarrely and lit the torch hanging just inside. He kept the match lit as he went around the room, lighting each of the hanging candles until the room was dimly lit. It was nothing like her room in appearance. The table, bed, and wash quarters were all there.

But there was a cave-like appearance to the room; she set her stuff on the table. The walls seemed to crowd in around her; the dancing lights from the lit candles intensified the smallness of the room.

There was a large bag, obviously filled with clothing, but what sat leaning in the corner truly drew her eye. It was a large axe like she had never seen. Much like her axe, this was not a tool; it was a weapon meant to cleave through flesh. The blade was nearly ten inches in height from the sharp point to the curved edge, and at the same length outward from the handle, the light from the torches danced on the blade. Made her question more than man's origins. She knew so little of his past besides that he had a connection with Hamilton Bastion.

Mia was still staring at the weapon when she felt his firsthand her waist. It was only a moment she felt the tightness of the bottom dress fall to her feet. Mia turned to stare at his bare chest. The light from the candles made his skin look darker. She raised her hands, digging her fingernails into him. She raked downward, following the white trail they left on his dark skin. There seemed to be nothing about his chest not perfect, not a scratch, out-of-place hair, or anything, and it mesmerized her.

Mia stood on the tip of her toes, still unable to reach his lips, until he met her with a soft kiss. She placed her free hand on his chin, so focused on his muscular face she stretched and at first kissed his perfect jawline and then playfully bit at him. She heard him groan as she let her hands once again find his chest sliding down his body, his hard abdomen, to the top of his ragged old pants. The thick leather belt slid free the moment she unlatched it, and his pants slid down his thick, muscular legs. Her eyes never left his as she pulled back, and again, he kissed her, placing a hand on the back of her head and pulling her into the embrace. Her undressing him, never the kiss. Her hands now lapped over his shoulders. He saw firsthand the back of her legs lifting her to his waist. She wrapped them tightly about his muscular waist as she felt the hand on her lower back holding her there with little effort, sending a rush of arousal over her entire body. There was no discomfort in his eyes from her weight. She smiled, leaning in for a kiss. As their lips released, his teeth tugged slightly at her lower lip before he set it free. Mia smiled. She couldn't stop smiling.

Gareth walked across the room with ease, not stopping until he turned, his back to the bed sitting on the edge. Mia rested her legs on his, sitting comfortably, her lips barely moving from his. She could taste each hot breath he exhaled. His hands slid up under her dress shirt, pulling, only slowing to pull free from her head and arms. The moment the cloth cleared, his lips were again there on hers. His hand traveled up her side and rested over her nipple; his massive hand engulfed her petite breast, firmly caressing her. Followed by his other doing the same to her other breast. Her dark nipples between his index and middle finger, he began to move them until she tried to pull away from the tender touch. She smiled as he released his grip. She pulled her body closer to his, kissing his lips, tasting his tongue. His body was immovable as she pressed against him, trying to close what little space there was between them. She wanted to feel herself pressed against his muscular frame and to feel every excited breath he took.

Gareth's arms enclosed around her, pulling her closer to his tight frame, more restricted than her corsets, causing her heart to race with excitement. Swift and certain, he twirled her over onto the bed. Mia, light-headed from the sudden movement, the softness of his bed on her back and head gave her a place to lay comfortably. He rested on his elbows, her arms and legs still wrapped around him. He pulled away to the point where she released the grip around his neck, laying there on the bed as he stood over her. His eyes wandered lustfully over her body. Only her boots remained on. Mia blushed. She raised, resting on her arms, her legs pressed slightly into him. She was not ashamed of her body, unlike the women she had spent most of her adult life around. Her people were not so hidden from the eye. People alike were comfortable in their skin. She bit on her lower lip as he lifted her left leg, pulling the boot free and tossing it over his shoulder to the floor with a hint of laughter. Then, the right boot in the same manner as the first. He still smiled as he raised her leg to his chest, kissing her ankle softly, his eyes never leaving hers.

Mia's other leg wrapped again around his large legs; her hands grabbed at the bed to pull her closer to him with no success. He laughed, looking down at her as he released her leg to the bed; he lowered his body down over her, his head over hers. Their eyes stuck on one another, and each breath tasted skin and chilled the sweat. Again, they kissed, wet and enthusiastic, as she reached to pull him down onto her, hands in his long black hair and her legs raised, wrapping around his, trying to pull him down closer to her. She wanted to feel his weight against her. He smiled. He was enjoying the tease. Her hands rested on his shoulders; her legs touched his hips. She smiled as he again pushed away from her, lowering his head to kiss her neck, then her collarbone. Her hands were still on his shoulders. She pushed her hips up into him as his wet, soft lips wrapped around her hard nipples. Mia gasped, arching her body into his. The only thing about the man she thought was soft was the tender touch of his lips. Each nipple as his hand caressed her breast, his mouth tasted her, and the entire time he looked up at her. She knew he wanted a reaction; she was fighting not to give him more than a smile, but she knew he could feel her body with each pleasurable shiver.

Mia's nails dug into his shoulders. She could feel the tearing of flesh under her fingers and the wet feel of blood. With each touch, her body ached. His mouth on her breasts, her nipples, she wanted more. A handful of hair, but again, he pulled away, her sweat-covered stomach as his tongue traced her belly button. His hands, one held her still on the flat of her stomach, not allowing her to move. His mouth was on the inside of her thigh with a gentle kiss, and she lost all her breath in a gasp. His hand removed from her stomach, and she sat up, feeling his tongue inside of her as she tightened her thighs around his head. She wrapped her legs around his head, and with handfuls of hair, she pulled him into her. His face on the inside of her thighs, she squeezed, wrapping her legs across her back as she fell back to her back, pushing her hips from the bed and into his face.

Mia slapped his head, trying to grab hair unsuccessfully, and then he stopped. Her eyes rolled as she struggled to catch her breath. She heard him; it was neither words nor a laugh. She looked up as she felt the bed shift with his weight once against her on the frame between her legs.

Gareth seemed to growl, hips lifted from the bed to hold her there with one hand. Mia gasped. Grabbing the bed sheets as she slowly pushed himself inside. Slowly and cautiously, he pushed himself in, pulling out, and each time, Mia trembled, releasing a small, lustful moan. She arched her hips into him, wanting more. Gareth made no noise. Instantly, she clasped her hand over her mouth, feeling him go deeper inside her, feeling his body looming over hers.

Gareth released her back to the bed, taking her hands into his, and he pulled her up to him as he sat. Still there, she rocked back and forth with him inside. She kissed and bit his lip and chin, trying to contain herself. It had been too long, far too long. Her body shook with each harsh avalanche of her body falling into his. He was still pulling her down with a free hand. The bed shook with each movement as their bodies danced with the lantern light.

Mia glared into his eyes. She leaned forward, pulling into him, close enough for her lips to whisper into his ear, "More." Gareth smiled as she pulled away, back to the bed where she fell. She wanted to smile, even laugh. He rolled her legs free as he turned her over onto her stomach. She rose to her hands and knees. She gritted her teeth, looking forward to feeling his hands tightly on her hips, even pushing back toward him. She sighed, feeling him again inside her, one hand on her hips, the other now pulling at her short hair. He pulled roughly until she sat up, her back against his body, one hand on her stomach and the other across his chest. The man was hard; everything about his body was solid, and it made her bite her lip just at the thought of him. He had slowed but kept his rhythm without the hard thrusts making the bed shake. He licked at her neck, shoulder, and ears, their bodies covered in sweat, his large fingers pulling and playing with her nipples. She reached back, pulling at his hair until their lips and tongues met. As she released, he smiled, pushing her back to the bed, both hands on her hips. He began to snap her hard back against him. Harder and harder, louder, and louder, at times, she thought it made Ulysses itself shake from his intensity. He growled with each passing scream and moan she couldn't contain. It only drove him to push harder, fuck harder. Her head in the covers, she reached back with her left hand, running her fingernails into his upper leg. She bit down on the covers; tighter, she gritted her teeth with each movement manufactured inside her.

Gareth stopped, pushing her to the bed and rolling her over onto her back. He lowered down onto her; Mia wrapped her legs around him, allowing him to lay onto her. Their bodies tangled with one another as he continued to force his will. Her body tensed and shook as he slowed with a groan.

She heaved her body close, kissing his forehead softly before she released her grip and fell back to the bed. Arms spread on the bed, she pulled at the sheets, but the man did not stop. A rhythm, his hips moving back and forth, her body arched against him for a second climax. He, too, slowed as another; a more intense groan escaped him as he rolled free of her.

Mia smiled as she tried to catch her breath.

Chapter Fifteen

January 1872

Logan Ezekiel sat on his horse, sleeves on his long white shirt rolled above his elbows, enjoying the rare warm winter sun. It was the first sunny day they had had in a week. He led his horse through the frozen mud to the edge of the solid water. "Can't pass here. The ice is too thin," he muttered, looking back at the others. Mia sat on top of a large, solid white horse. A pale green dress with a matching jacket was the closest to him.

"The buck did," a big, burly man said. He wore a fur coat with a thick fur neck, keeping the cold out. His thick beard was trimmed neatly, and his dark hair was beginning to thin from age. He slid off his horse, tied it off, and pointed toward the trail.

"Too risky with the horses, Benson," Logan stated, turning to the man. He saw the look in the other man's eyes; he intended to leave the horses behind.

"We have been following this buck for nearly a day. We can't let a little thin ice slow us down," before anything else could be said. Mia and Jean, dressed in similar dresses to the other women, were both off their horses and tied to the same tree.

"Reach me the reigns," a third man called out. "There should be a shallow passing downstream. I'll take them and catch up with you. Maybe even run the trophy back to you in the process."

"Sure, Eli?" Logan questioned. The third man sat high on his horse, the biggest of all the animals, and was well cared for. It was obvious the man took pride in his horse and did not intend to leave it alone. His graying handlebar mustache distracted others from the scar on his neck; he wore a hat that seemed too big for his head. The rest of his clothing was a pale brown color. A long duster jacket hid most of his wardrobe.

"You know I am," he said with a smile, taking all the reigns. None of the group moved until they saw he was clear.

Benson led down to the ice. He was the heaviest of the group and the first to cross. One by one, they reached the other side. He stood at the top of the bank, hands-on-hips, when he turned to look at the others. "Where is Mia?"

Each of the three looked around, not seeing the other woman. It was Jean who spotted her. Slinking off through the underbrush, paying little attention to the pristine dress she was wearing, the light green almost blending with the dead winter forest. She was armed with a handmade hickory bow with stone-tipped arrows. "I hate it when she does that," Benson said with a smile as he took Logan's hand and helped him to his feet at the top of the bank.

"Why? Cause she is a better hunter than the both of us?" Logan questioned as he turned to help Jean up as well.

"Exactly," Benson said with a hearty laugh. "She can see the path the deer took from way over there, and I have to be right on top of it with my failing eyes."

"Old age, my friend, it is unkind," Logan stated as he followed behind Benson down the deer's trail.

Benson followed the trail with Logan and Jean directly behind him. They, at times, lost sight of the other woman. But Logan continued to look for her more than the buck they tracked. They traveled nearly a mile when they heard movement ahead. The doe leaped from the clearing and only starred at them. Benson raised his rifle, aiming, but did not fire. There was still movement in the brush behind the deer.

The whistle of an arrow cut through the air; they all heard it even from there. Followed close by the crash of a large animal running through the brush. The buck broke through as a second arrow pierced through the side of the animal. He crashed headfirst into the path in front of them. The doe was gone, Benson approaching the large ten-point buck lowering down to lift its head from the ground. They looked up just as Mia stepped through the brush. "Well done," Benson said with a smile.

Mia smiled, placing an arrow back on its quiver. "We will have a nice meal tonight," Logan looked around at everyone as he approached his wife, and they kissed. He left a tight grip at her side, pulling her as close as the dress would allow.

Logan moved through the woods. He was unarmed and kept a cautious look at the wilderness around him. "Mia," he said aloud, soft enough so he didn't scare even the scarcest of a nearby animal. They had returned home from the hunt, and Mia disappeared almost immediately. He knew where she went when she wanted to be alone.

The crackle of the fire and the smell of the smoke told him how close he was. He crept forward. It was then he saw her. She sat on the ground with her legs crossed by the low burning fire. He was accustomed to leaving her alone when she drifted away from home; it was Jean who told him he should. That he should give her space when she needed it. They had been married for four years. He could tell something bothered her on the ride back home; she had even taken a souvenir from the kill. One side of the bucks' antlers was a first for her. "There you are," he said, stepping out into the clearing. She was still in the light green top; the long shirt was modified. She had cut the sides of the shirt at her hips. The bottom of her dress hung by a nearby tree, and she was barefoot.

"Sorry," Mia said, staring intently at the fire.

"Nothing to be sorry for. I was just worried," he said, approaching. He took a seat by the fire but on the opposite side, trying not to crowd her. He could tell the small area had been her most frequent retreat. He could imagine that in the summer, it was a beautiful spot with a small natural waterfall no more than five feet high that made for wonderful viewing. Now, it was frozen, and the once-flowing water was stuck in a constant fall. It was how he felt when he looked at her, constantly falling for her. He looked across the fire, and the light danced in her eyes. He often wondered if she absolutely loved him, as they had known each other for such a brief period. And for that time, he was more an expert than a

suitor. Again, he glanced at the waterfall. Was that how she felt? Like she was frozen in a moment of falling? His frown couldn't be hidden as he looked at the fire. After so many years, they seemed almost perfect, but the thoughts were still there. Did she miss her former life? He was sure she did, but she did love him. Did she love the life he had come to provide for her? He saw the antler, broken in shape with several of the tines missing.

Logan saw the axe; she had often kept it hidden from him. It was something he had taken from the field of the battle; it was her weapon. He had even been the one to give it to her the day after their marriage. He thought she should have it to remember her former life; he did not want to take that away from her. Just wanted her to love him. More now than ever, he looked around, and the thoughts crept in.

Logan looked at her and again at the axe, the ten-inch handle hand-carved with notches and designs, but he had no clue about their meaning. He had always wanted to ask but never had the nerve. He never had the nerve to ask her about her youth; only once did he ask her her real name. It was Jean who chose Mia; her tutor knew her given name, but he never pressed any more on either. It was their secret. In time, maybe she would want him to know. Small, thin, leather straps used to tie the weapon to the wielder cling to the handle, a sharp blade no more than four inches in length with more designs on the handle holding it in place. Each mark held meaning to the wielder, and he was sure that was why he kept it. No one else knew he swept it from the field the day. Even before he knew she would be accompanying him, he intended to keep it. Like the white feather, the small item now hanging around Mia's neck, he looked at her. It was there, and it turned his frown into a smile. Maybe she did love him, or the feather meant more to her than just something given to her by her "master." He couldn't fight back the ill thoughts in his mind. Was he no better than the old men in the South who kept men and women as slaves because of the color of their skin?

"What are you thinking?" Mia questioned, smiling; her bare feet stretched out near the flame.

"Huh?" Logan paused. He didn't want to answer. He never wanted her to know he doubted her.

"Whenever you are deep in thought, your forehead... it creases, makes you look like your father," Mia replied. He smiled. He remembered the look well, but when his father's forehead creased, it was normally out of anger and not deep thoughts. It was the look he held often after he learned his son intended to marry some Indian instead of a good English girl.

"I don't know what you mean," he said with a coy smile. He looked away from her, and his smile grew bigger.

He only looked back when he saw her shadow grow; she stood and walked over to him. He stretched out his legs as she sat in his lap. On his legs, she pulled his chin to look into her eyes. "What are you thinking, husband?"

"I am thinking how lucky I am to have you as my wife," he quickly replied, his hands resting on her hips as she stretched her arms out, letting her hands clasp around the back of his neck where she started to twirl his hair in her fingers.

"You need a haircut," she stated with a smile, looking at his growing brown hair. Her hair was nearly down to the middle of her back now.

"I think this is the longest I have ever seen your hair," he said with a smile. She bit her lip and almost immediately looked away. "The hunt today, you were something else."

"I am at home in the woods," she said, looking at the trees above. The sky was clear, but the wind had a chill to it that even the small fire near them couldn't fend off.

"I know, we should spend more time out here," he said, enjoying the view. "Or maybe do some traveling; there are expeditions and travelers every day going west. See the States and all its wonder."

She unclasped her hands and now rested them on her shoulders. "And how would they react, seeing a white man married to a red skin." She looked down.

"Don't talk like that. You know it doesn't matter to me what anyone says," he replied.

"Not everyone is like you, Logan," Mia stated.

"Trust me." He placed a finger under her chin. She had started to look away from him, but now their eyes once again connected. "It will be wonderful." Their foreheads collapsed in on one another softly.

"I do trust you, husband," she whispered, kissing him softly. Once again, her hands were clasped behind his neck, messing with his hair.

The chill in the air picked up, and the first drizzle felt like snow, which would be before the night was over. They never moved, still embraced. "Maybe we should go inside?"

"No," she whispered, looking more at his lips than his eyes now. Again, she kissed him.

"I'm glad fate brought us together," he muttered between kisses. She smiled and sat away from him for a moment. The rain had started to become steadier.

"You talk too much," she said with a smile, pulling into him with another kiss. Her body pulled closer to his. She only wore a thin shirt. His hands rested on her hips. Hers

traveled slowly down the vest, taking time to unbutton each button carefully, and then came the shirt as she repeated her actions.

When the last button came to lose, she pulled the shirt from his shoulders and lowered it to kiss his neck. He had leaned back and rested on his outstretched arms. She kissed his neck, then his shoulder, then his chest as her hands slowly dragged down his pale arms.

She slowly kissed his shoulder, then leaned her head into him, and steadily, she sat there breathing before she pulled away to look at him. "Let's do it, let's go… somewhere, anywhere. Back to England if we must. I need to go someplace… else. We have been here four years, this cramped place, even the wilderness has grown old to me. I need to go someplace fresh, wild."

"Wild?" he questioned with a smile. She grinned big with him.

"I don't care, just let's go… tomorrow," she stated.

"Let's not get too ahead of ourselves," he replied, "We'll discuss this tomorrow. I am sure Benson knows some wild and exciting places we could go to. He has been all over the world and has seen some strange and exciting places, he tells me." He reached and wiped the rain drop from the tip of her nose.

Mia leaned forward again, pressing her body into him and softly kissing his lips. Arms wrapped around his neck, pulling the two of them as close as they could be. His hands were firmly around her back, holding her tight. The rain began to pour as she raised her chin to let it splash across her face. Logan's lips were on her neck, and he kissed softly, paying little attention to the rain now. She leaned further away from him, enjoying the rain. As she did, he lowered, kissing her breasts and hard nipples through her half-wet shirt. He again started to kiss her neck, then her chin as she leaned into him, pushing him back to the ground, their lips and tongues dancing. She smiled, biting her lower lip at his face, a face full of surprise at her action.

"I love you," he leaned forward, whispering in her ear. Slowly, their eyes glued on one another and their hands on each other. She bit down on her lower lip as she pressed her body against hers.

"And I love you," she whispered as she quickly kissed him, pushing him back to the surface behind. It was no longer hard from the frozen winter, wet from the rain. He looked to the dark sky above, the full moon she sat on him. The first snowflake he saw he felt float and land on his chin, then another and another as the rain turned to snow. He pushed off the ground, lifting her into the air. The two of them smiled

as he packed her closer to the fire. Mia was a small woman, but each step came slower and slower until he was comfortably near the fire. Lowering the two of them down, he set her softly to the wet ground. They lay intertwined near the dying fire, snow still falling around them. Logan pulled Mia close to him, her eyes shut. She seemed truly at peace here.

• • •

Hours had passed since Logan left to find Mia; everyone knew he had left, but it was Benson sitting outside, waiting for his wife to return with him at his side. They both smiled at each other, soaked to the bone but genuinely happy. Benson smiled, too, and as they walked up to the door, he stood. They had not even seen the new horse on the porch; they had even walked within feet of him to get to the steps. "We have company," Benson stated.

Logan did not stop smiling as he answered, "At this time of day? Who came calling?" He continued to look into his wife's eyes.

"A Sir Alistair Crawford insisted on waiting, been here for a while. Said it was of some importance," Benson stated.

"Do you know this man?" Mia questioned.

Logan's confused expression said it all. "I went to school with him years ago. I did not even realize he was in the States," he left his wife's side, rushing into the house.

Jean sat by the fire with a teacup and saucer in hand. When Logan stepped into the room, he saw the man sitting opposite the young woman's chair. Bright red short but curly hair, a full red beard, and a coy smile waiting for him with his cup. He stood immediately. "Ah, sight for sore Scottish eyes," the man called, wearing a faded gray suit with a tie. A small, brimmed hat of the same color sat on the arm of the chair; he walked across the room to greet the man with an open hand.

"Alistair, what are you doing here?" Logan questioned. He was still in shock to see an old friend so far from his home country.

"Always to the point, what kept me so focused in our school days," he turned smiling at Jean, who blushed when the man looked at her. "I was just telling your young friend here about our days in university, you, Hamilton, and myself. Ah, the times we used to have. The drinking, the women…" The man paused as he saw Mia. "Excuse my manners, ma'am." He bowed, and Mia gave a polite bow as well. "Was told she was ah beauty, but I did not quite expect a goddess," he said, grinning, crossing the room and taking Mia's hand

for a kiss. Mia looked to Logan, who watched his friend close, still with a questioning, shocked haze in his eyes.

"Thank you," she stated.

"What are you doing in the states, Alistair?" Logan questioned. The man still looked into Mia's eyes.

"I could get lost in those," he said with a grin.

"Alistair... quit flirting with my wife," Logan said, putting an arm across the other man's shoulders.

"Cannot help it. She is exquisite," Alistair stated.

Alistair again leaned, kissing Mia's hand. He looked at Logan through the corner of his eyes and smiled as his lips touched her skin. "It is a pleasure," he looked to Mia and then to Jean, "to meet the both of you surrounded by beautiful women, my old friend." He turned to face Logan yet again, smiling from ear to ear, but Logan had lost his smile. "Ah, sour puss, this is why you were no fun at university. You and Hamilton are both always so serious."

"I suppose now you intend to tell me why you are here?" he questioned, holding out his hand, and the two shook.

"Guess I can, maybe in private or in front of your beautiful wife. All is the same to me," Alistair stated, walking across the room and taking a seat again across from Jean.

"Anything you have to say to me, you can say to Mia," Logan stated, crossing the room, Jean stood and joined Mia and Benson at the door.

"Not so much what I have to say, but I have a letter for you." He reached into the inside of his jacket and pulled out a letter, reaching it across to Logan as he took his seat.

"From Hamilton?" Logan questioned, glaring at the outside of the letter. The bad handwriting was recognizable to him.

"Ah," is all Alistair said, sitting back in his chair and looking across the room at the others with a smile. Logan read the letter silently as he sat comfortably in his chair.

"Dear Friend,

I hope this letter finds you and your lovely new wife in good help, Logan. I was surprised to hear you took the young Indian to wed. The truth is I never thought you would find the one to truly marry. But from what Mason has said, she is a spitfire and near perfect for you. You always seemed to want someone to create chaos in your life. No doubt the new addition pleased your parents and the entire nose-in-the-air English men and stuffy women back home. I believe that is why you spent so much time with Alistair and me when we were there. We were different. A

Scott and an American… we were quite the three, weren't we…?

By now, you are sitting there reading, wishing I would get to the point, your nose probably twitching from the annoyance. I swear the only time you ever had patience was with the women, like the crazy red head Scottish one Alistair introduced you to…

To the point, I get, it has been nearly ten years since we have seen each other face-to-face. I want to change that. I need you to come to Washington and accompany Alistair here as soon as you read this letter. My friend, the future is coming, and the wondrous ideas I see will come true in my lifetime. I want you to be a part of it all.

I met a man, Stephen Beck, a genius, I tell you. I never throw the word around, this, you know. You will have to meet him… It is important, Logan. You will not regret making this trip.

-	**Hamilton Bastion"**

Logan folded the letter and lounged in his chair; he stared off at the fire to his left before he glanced at Alistair, who was sitting in a similar position. He smiled at the man, leg crossed across the other. "What is Hamilton up to?" Logan questioned.

"Bloody hell if I know, my letter had your letter enclosed in it asking me to come here and deliver yours. I am as much in the dark as you," Alistair stated. "But it is bloody exciting, isn't it?"

Logan glanced back at the others still standing at the door, Mia now approached, and neither broke their gaze until she stood at the side of the chair. "What is it?" Mia questioned.

"Hamilton wants me to come to Washington," Logan stated.

"You should go. He would not have sent the letter if it was not important," Mia stated, looking across to Alistair.

"Lady is as smart as she is, beautiful lad," Alistair stated with a grin, his elbows resting on the arms of the chair and clasped together in front of his face.

"What of... of our trip?" Logan questioned.

"Go to Washington. When you come back, we will go someplace, any place," Mia stated, leaning down and kissing him on the forehead.

Logan sat tall on his horse, looking back at his home and, more importantly, at his wife standing on the steps. His bags were on the horse, and Alistair sat on his steed just a few feet away.

"Train will not wait on us, Logan," Alistair stated, breaking the man from his haze.

Logan turned his horse and trotted back to the steps. He jumped from his steed, picked Mia from the ground, and twirled her around. "You can come with me," he stated.

"Go, see your friend. I will be waiting here for you," she replied as he set her back to the ground. She held him close and whispered into his ear, "Meghana." Logan did not have to question what she had said. It was her name, her birth-given name she had guarded so hard from others.

"Kiss me again before you go," Mia said, leaning into him with her head on his chest. He did not even question what it meant; he quickly kissed, a tight hug and a final smile. He remounted his horse and rode up to his friend, saying nothing as the two-headed off to Washington.

• • •

Alistair Crawford smiled. Logan was not quick to return the smile. They had been sitting in the room alone for nearly an hour. They were forced to wait on the man who had sent word for them to come to Washington, their former schoolmate and friend Hamilton Bastion. "At least the tea is decent," Alistair said as he raised his cup.

"He asks us to come here and then makes us wait once we have traveled so far... not like Hamilton," Logan stated, standing and looking out the window. They were on the outskirts of Washington, far from the bustle of the busy government-run city. "What do you suppose is in that building." He looked back over his shoulder. The building is set by its lonesome, with several guards surrounding it. "Big enough to house... I don't know," he said with a smile. The building was four stories high, the best he could tell from their position in the house.

They heard boots in the hall, the door crept open, and in stepped a young soldier in his full military wear with a saber at his side. "Mr. Ezekiel, Mr. Crawford," he said with a bow. "Can you come with me?"

"Where is Hamilton?" Logan quickly questioned.

"He is waiting for you," the soldier replied.

"We have been waiting for ourselves," Logan stated as he turned and picked up his jacket from the chair. Alistair placed an arm on his shoulder as they walked out behind the soldier, who said nothing more.

He led them from the building to another, smaller or less distinguished home across the road from the one they wanted.

The soldier led them through a series of doors until he knocked at a big double door. "Come," a voice called out. The soldier opened the door and let the two men enter, but the soldier did not.

"Logan, Alistair, I do apologize for making you wait," Hamilton Bastion stated. "It has been far too long since I have seen your youthful faces," he said with a chuckle. He was a year younger than both. He wore a white shirt as it stuck to his body from the hot room where they now stood. He turned to look at them, and a hearty smile graced his face. "You can leave," he stated to a fact. For a moment, the two men both thought he was telling them, not seeing the mountain of a man in the opposite corner of the room. Long black hair pulled back into a ponytail, he wore a suit that looked a size too small for his frame, and both men stared as if he looked like something out of a book. A head taller than either, he

gave a bow as he passed them and left the room. Both looked to the door for a moment before going back to Hamilton.

"Hired muscle, Hamilton? Seems serious," Alistair stated.

"Gareth is his name. He comes someplace overseas like the two of you, but I find having him around discourages anyone from causing trouble," Hamilton stated.

"The size of the man…" Alistair stated as he turned to look at Hamilton.

"Why are we here, Hamilton?" Logan quickly questioned.

"To the point, Logan, as always," he replied with a smile. "I need friends, to be perfectly honest, I need people I can trust, and I think outside of my dear brothers, I trust no one more than the two of you."

"Flattered, really, but you said this was urgent. We come to Washington," Logan stated eagerly.

"I hate to agree with Logan's impatience, but we did come all the way here, and you had us wait for an hour before you brought us here," Alistair stated. He had unbuttoned his jacket and taken a seat across the desk from Hamilton.

"I am sorry for the wait, truly, I am, but I was in a meeting and could not rush," Hamilton stated. He stood, walked over to a wooden cabinet, undid the lock, and reached *inside, pulling out some rolled-up papers. "This is why I wanted you to come to Washington. And it is why I am going to ask for your trust, silence, and loyalty from this day forth. We are on the cusp of history, my friends; the future is now."*

Both men looked to one another and then back to the other as he set the papers on the desk. "I ask for a commitment of possibly years. If you don't believe you can do so... I will ask you to leave now with no hard feelings." Logan turned and started to the door, stopping with his hand on the handle. He took a deep breath before he turned back to him. Alistair smiled when Logan turned back to them.

"I have a young wife, Hamilton. Do you realize what it is you ask of me?" Logan stated.

"I do, and the moment you are settled, I will send her and anyone else to accompany them to your location. By this, I promise," Hamilton replied. He rolled the papers out on the desk, and the two men walked over to look at designs for a ship on the front page. Both looked at it in wonderment, lost in what they were seeing. "I have purchased..." There was a pause in his speech. "I have a production facility in Montana. One is very much like the one on these very grounds, and I want the two of you to head up the project there. To build this."

"And I am to take it one is already being built here?" Logan questioned.

"Early stages, to be called the Ulysses," he replied.

"After Grant," Alistair said with a smile.

"I also assume only a few people know about this second... ship," Logan questioned.

"I fear people are attempting to stop our production. Even now, in the preliminary stages, there are whispers," Hamilton replied, leaving the papers on the table as he approached the window. "You will leave in two days, with a caravan of others heading west where you will slip off from the group heading north without little question. Everything from supplies to your transport has been arranged. My brother Mason will be with you, as will several others, people I trust with what you will be doing."

Logan and Alistair both circled the desk to get a better look at the plans. "Marvelous," Alistair stated, looking back at Hamilton.

"Sure, it is not just paranoia," Logan questioned.

"Two days ago, a carrier with sensitive documents was hung from a tree two miles from here. I know I am asking a lot of you, Logan, about the both of you. But I think you see now this is bigger than just us," he stated with a big smile as

they both turned back to look at the papers. Their minds were already made up.

• • •

Logan sat, cigar in the mouth as he watched from the balcony of the home where he and Alistair were first forced to wait. He watched the building; there were a lot of travelers in and out of the complex, but he had yet to see the inside. Hamilton had asked them not to press, to stay clear of the building, and to try to stay anonymous for the two days they would be there. Logan knew the tone his old friend had, worrisome and anxious as if it was left up to him, he would have shuffled them off to Montana the moment they arrived in Washington.

A knock came at the door. He turned just as the same young soldier from before exited out to the balcony. He stood there for a moment, letting another exit before retreating into the home.

Logan knew immediately it was a woman. He stood out of respect; she lifted her hood from her eyes, and Logan paused as he saw Viva, Mason's sister-in-law. Her blond hair pulled up into a bun, she smiled her mischievous grin. "Viva," he said with a bow before he sat. In his mind, he could still see her naked frame from when she threw herself at him, married or not.

"It is nice to see you, Logan," she said, approaching the banister and turning her back to look at him. She untied the cloak and tossed it to the chair at Logan's side.

"Wish I could say the same," Logan retorted.

"No hard feelings from before, I hope," she raised her hand, showing the ring on her finger. "I am a happily married woman now." Her smile never changed; it was the same smile from the day in the barn when she suggested keeping Mia as a servant if she was called his wife.

"Congratulations," Logan said with an empty tone.

"Thank you," she replied with a smile. She arched her chest forward as she adjusted the dress off her shoulders. She smiled at Logan when she noticed him watching. "He is a young soldier, a military man. You will come to know him soon. Not as goal oriented as you, from wealth and intelligence. But I thought it past time waiting on others to come to their senses." She smiled wickedly at Logan, and he looked at her questioning. "Yes, Mr. Ezekiel, we will be accompanying you and the Scottish man to Montana with Mason." Her smile grew larger as she looked at the man, sending a chill up his back.

The woman looked at the door as if she was waiting for something. Logan flicked the cigar out into the dirt, and almost immediately, she moved. Before he could make any move, she was there in front of him, pulling the dress up as she sat straddling his lap, leaning forward with her large cleavage in his face. Logan sat back, hands on her hips, holding her at reach, "I am still available to you though, Mr. Ezekiel," she stated, forcing a kiss onto him. Her tongue was in his mouth before she moved away. "We will get to know each other much better in the days, even months to come." She pulled the shoulders of her dress back over her exposed skin. Viva smiled and blew him a kiss; she was gone as quickly as she arrived.

Logan sat on his horse alone, and he was leagues ahead of the rest of the caravan. Another horse trotted up to catch him; there was a scout still out in front of them, but no one near close enough for anyone to hear. "The Viva woman is a firecracker,' Alistair stated, giving a glance back at the caravan.

"You have no idea," Logan replied with a smile.

"Missing Mia?" Alistair questioned.

"Since the moment my lips left hers," he stated with a smile, and Alistair laughed. "I left a letter with Hamilton for him to have delivered to her when he sends for her to join us."

"Ah, my good friend, you will see her again, I promise you," Alistair said, reaching out and giving a friendly slap to his back.

"I hope you are right, friend," he stated, looking back at the caravan of people behind them. "But I have my fears."

Chapter Sixteen

Mia woke. Eyes wide as she stared at the unfamiliar ceiling, she thought vividly of the last time she and Logan made love. The night before he left for Washington, they put their plans for traveling on hold, possibly forever. She felt Gareth's lumbering arm lay across her stomach. His hot breath on her bare neck. She twisted under his arm to look into his closed eyes. She slowly tried to pull out from under him by sliding off the bed so as not to disturb him. Mia stopped at the edge, looking for her clothing. His hand latched onto her wrist, pulling her back to the bed and on top of him before either could speak.

"Going somewhere?" he questioned.

Mia felt his tight grip on her hips. There was no opportunity for her to answer as their lips met. Mia pushed him to a sitting position on his hips. It was hard to ignore what she was feeling, both emotionally and physically. He sat up against her, her hands on his bare chest. She again blushed.

She could feel his excitement. His heart raced under her fingertips; she felt her own do the same. She kissed him; she had wanted to slip away unnoticed, but now she couldn't help it. What was first a small peck was now a lingering, wet kiss… she pulled away, resting her head on his shoulder. She wanted him as badly as he wanted her. "What is it?" he questioned.

She sat up, looking at him, hands still on his chest, and there was the smile. Not unlike Logan's but different, it was no half-smile, but his entire face lit up as they looked at each other. His long dark hair, dark eyes, and thick lips. His dark skin was not unlike her natural color, his dark eyes, and his full grin, so she had to turn away. Looking into his eyes was not helping her will to flee. The touch of his fingers pushed a wild strand of hair from her face, bringing her crashing back to look into his eyes. She could not decide who was the hunted here; everything about the brute of a man excited her. There had been times she had thought she heard an accent in his voice, undistinguishable, or at least she could not place it. And yet she knew little except he had a connection with Hamilton Bastion. She shyly smiled. Did he also know her husband, Logan? The thought brought her smile crashing into a frown as she returned the favor, pushing hair from his face. She had also realized his hair was now longer than her own.

"What is wrong?" Gareth again questioned.

"Nothing is wrong," she lied. The only physical contact between the two still caused her heart to race. She could feel his manhood there, so close; no one could blame her for a repeat of the night before. But unlike then, she was not high on adrenaline. She was thinking more clearly now. And the man she had made love to the night before was not who she now thought of.

"You have the look?" Gareth said. He still sat up but leaned back on his arms.

"What look is that?" she questioned, looking away.

"You regret what we did," he asked. He released his weight and leaned back on the bed, placing his hands behind his head. She stared at his arms, and for a moment, she thought about letting him have her again. To have him tower over her, his arms having her caged in under him.

"No," she said after hesitation.

"You are thinking about your husband," Gareth questioned. He said it so casually.

"Sorry," Mia stated.

"Maybe it is I who should apologize," he said again, sitting up. He moved out from under her with ease. He pulled his pants up, and she only paused when she saw the long, fresh scratches down his back. They would not be scarred, but she smiled on seeing them. He turned back to look before picking his shirt up and started to button it.

"I am sorry," she said again, shifting to the other end of the bed.

As she sat there staring at his things, the large axe, she almost didn't see him approach, not stopping until he was in front of her. Mia didn't want to look at him; she was afraid of seeing the disappointment in his eyes. But he was still smiling. It would be easy for her to reach out and pull the man back into bed. Simple, just reach for him, he no doubts would have obliged.

Gareth leaned down until the two were on eye level; he extended forward, kissing her on the forehead before returning to her gaze. "I will not pressure you," he said, standing. "There is a lot about me you don't know. As there is a lot about you, I don't know. But we have time." He felt the room. It was his room, but she was sure he was off to work or to eat.

Mia again locked her eyes on the large weapon; she slowly stood and crossed the room, moving the bags from the long handle. The axe, blade, and all were nearly as tall as her at five feet. She placed her petite hand on the handle just below the blade, pulling it from the corner where it sat. The axe was heavier, even heavier than she had imagined. Why would he have such a weapon? It then crossed her mind, what if Gareth… the man she had just had sex with hours before, was the person sent to kill the child. She set the blade down, turning to survey the rest of the room. 'Frost, it was Frost," she whispered out loud in a self-convincing voice before she crossed the room, picking her shirt up and putting it on. She quickly slipped her boots on. Picked up the rest of her things and left for her room.

Mia dressed, but still, she lay on her bed staring at the ceiling, thinking about Logan and Gareth. The two were colliding in her mind, two vastly different men. Logan was small in stature but always thinking and considering others before himself.

There was a soft knock on her door. She sat up. "Gareth," she whispered, unable to fight back the smile or the word she blurted out.

"I am sorry to disappoint," William Beck said with a fake smile on his lips.

"Sorry," Mia muttered, shifting her legs off the bed and standing, wiping the crease from the dress to make it more suitable.

"Julian wishes to speak to you," Beck stated as he stepped out into the hall. Mia walked to the hallways and started in one direction when she realized he was not following. "He is on the viewing deck." She smiled if he had made it to the deck where he was recovering.

Beck shook his head slightly when he saw the smile, his eyes filled with sorrow. He led her up the stairs and outside, where he remained at the door.

Mia approached the railing; the sun was powerful, and she could tell it had reached nearly midday. Julian leaned against the railing; his weight rested on the wooden structure. Immediately, she realized he wore no mask as he glanced back at her. He showed no emotion on seeing her. His beard was much thicker than the day before and uneven.

"You wanted to see me?" Mia questioned.

Julian glanced at her again and then back out into the light. It was easy to see he had lost a lot of weight in just a few days. His eyes seemed hollow, and his lips, a tint of blue, parted and quivered like a man more than twice his age. "I always thought I would die in some fevered battle, outnumbered by hordes of savages or rebels, who knew. It was the way I wanted to go. I know how that sounds; no one wants to die, but at one time, I wished I would go out by the sword. Or an axe, a blade all the same." He turned and looked at Mia with a half-smile.

"You are not dying," Mia stated.

"I am, and I know it. You know everyone on this vessel knows it. Smith did what possibly thousands of others wanted to do, but only a frail young girl ever came close to doing." He smiled, lowering his face but not looking at anything. "Tomorrow, we set down in Colorado, two days after that San Francisco."

The man started to cough, his hand to his mouth, and it went on for over a minute. With each hack, it got louder, and she could tell he was having a problem catching his breath. Finally, he regained his breath. He pulled it clear of his mouth, and the dark red blood covered the palm of his hand. He smiled when he saw it; he was bleeding internally, and he knew it. "I feel it crawling inside me; whatever it was he gave me, it is tearing me up inside bad. Beck's father..." He glanced back at William, who remained at the door. "Two days to die, I'm on day number three..."

Mia stood with her arms crossed tightly against her chest, watching him weave back and forth in the wind. He moved slowly and grunted with each subtle movement from the pain he was in. "You should be in bed," Mia stated, taking a step toward him. He looked at her with an odd smile, one of honest hope and happiness.

"I always thought I would die in some fevered battle, outnumbered by hordes of savages or rebels, who knows. I was the way I wanted to go…" he realized he had said the same thing already and smiled. "Repeating myself now, look out, Mia… did you think you would ever see anything so marvelous?" They could see the Rocky Mountains and the high snowy peaks as the sun bounced around the edges. "More beautiful than any battle I have ever witnessed."

Mia looked back to William and then back to Julian. He was now looking at her again. "I think I want to spend a few hours at the helm one last time." It was as if William had heard him and approached.

The two of them helped Julian from the viewing deck, through the mess hall, and down the two flights of stairs back to the helm of the Ulysses. They helped him sit back at the helm, the captain's chair, and he smiled almost the moment he melted into the seat.

Mia stood at the back of the room when Beck joined her. "Is there any chance he will live?"

"He is a fighter, already surpassed my father, and he has gotten some color back today…the sun did him some good," Beck looked at him and then back to Mia.

"I need to see Frost's room," she stated.

"I thought you would,' Beck reached into his pocket, pulled out a key, and turned to leave toward the stairs. Mia took a last glance at Julian before she followed along.

Beck let her into the room alone. The first thing she noticed was that it was the room of a persistent man of routine. The bed was made to perfection; a small chest at the end of the bed had a lock on it, and there was nothing in the room out of place. She turned back to the door and shut it behind her as she crossed the room. She smashed the lock on the chest with her axe, breaking it free. She started to claw and dig into the chest, throwing anything and everything to the floor around her. She did not stop until she got to the bottom of the chest and found nothing. Nothing suspicious. She pulled the covers from the bed and pushed the mattress from its frame. And again, nothing. She ran her hands through her hair, frustrated and breathing heavily and uncontrolled. Three days out of port, a brief time...

Mia exited the room and immediately realized the door across from his was open. She placed her hand on the door and gave it a push. She saw nothing but knew immediately whose room it was. William Beck's room, the most noticeable thing of the room, was the smell. With the smell of paper, the room was littered with books all around. Thick, small, new books of all sorts, slowly she walked into the room, careful not to step on any of the number of leather-bound books. This is what she needed; she knew Gareth's room, the large mysterious axe in the corner. Frost's near-perfect put-together room, and now in Beck's. She surveyed the entire room, a pile of clothes she pushed her foot through until she had seen to the floor. Again, she turned and looked through the books, and nothing. Nothing would even lead her to believe Beck could do what she was thinking.

Mia exited Beck's room and approached Stone's and then Smith's. Both doors were locked. She needed to investigate both rooms. But first, she needed a way in. Smith posed no threat to her ward. No one was going to let him out of his cell. Same with Owens, he would remain in his cell for the remainder of the trip.

Stone, the teddy bear of a man, was a more immediate threat. Like several of the others, she knew little about him except his smile. He was always smiling; even after the events in the town, he still managed to smile. She entered the room and saw Beck standing near the captain's chair. She could see Julian still there in his seat, and she could hear his wheezing breath even from the door. She approached the chair; the moment Julian saw her, he looked at Beck. "Can you give us a minute?" Mia watched as the tall black man left her to a man she had wished death on past occasions, and now that she saw him mostly wasting away, she felt sorry for him. "Something I need to tell you, Mia, something you need to keep to yourself until after you have landed in California."

"We, until after we have landed in California," she quickly stated, and Julian smirked at her forwardness. Though she was sure he could see the sorrow for his condition in her eyes.

"So be it," he said after a couple of coughs. "Kent Hardy is not who he says he is. I do not know how I missed it before. But the man is not who we thought."

"Sophia," Mia grew pale, thinking about how much she was leaving the little girl with the man.

"Is safe, safer than she is probably in your presence, but he needs to know you know. He trusts you with the girl but not with his identity. Go speak with him," Julian stated, turning to look forward out the viewing glass again. He took a deep breath, almost the breath of a healthy man without the long wheeze as a combination.

Mia left the room but did not head to see Hardy and Sophia. If Julian said he was lying but could still be trusted, she would have to believe him for now. Hardy would have to answer the question soon. She marched down the stairs to the third floor; she had lifted the keys to the cells when she was in the viewing room. Now, she had a question for Smith, and it did not pertain to Sophia. She stepped to the door; the man was huddled in a corner, lying on the floor in a fetal position. She watched him for a moment, and it almost seemed like he was not breathing. She put the key into the hole and almost immediately she saw the big man rise from the floor. His right hand huddled and wrapped against his body. She slowly turned the key, and it seemed to take a minute before the light from the hall poured into the cell. The large man covered his eyes. "You," he muttered. He did not try to stand but pulled his hand closer to his body.

Mia let the handle of the axe slide down her grip until she felt the large bundle of leather strapping on the end. The man flinched when he saw it and turned his head away with his eyes closed. She could see the fear. He expected her to kill him.

"Took a long time for the old man to die," he muttered, shaking.

"Julian isn't dead," she stated. His head turned quickly toward her; his mouth opened in amazement. "His breathing is returning to normal…" The large man's jaw clenched in anger; it was the reaction Mia was hoping for.

The man pushed off his good hand until he was in a standing position. "He should have been dead a day or even two ago, shouldn't he? You were giving him the poison over the days, possibly from the moment you began to cook and deliver his breakfast in the mornings. You could not risk him getting sick too soon. The old bastard is going to live." He reached out with his good hand, and the smack of the blunt side of her axe echoed through the hall. The man retreated in pain, pulling his good hand against his body.

"There is going to come a day I'll get my hands on you," Smith said with a growl.

Mia smiled and looked down at the man. She took a step toward him, and he slid down the wall until he was secured on the floor again. "I will be waiting, and on that day," she held the sharp edge up to show the man, "I will not be using the blunt end." She turned to Owens's cell. "We'll be landing in a few days, and you'll be set free." The kid looked well, considering his situation. She turned to leave the hall.

• • •

Mia stood with her hand on the doorknob; it was the door going in the opposite direction of where she should be. She opened it, and the warm air, more suffocating than anywhere else on the ship, blew through her. The smell of horses and steam choked her up, almost taking her breath away. Slowly, she crawled down the stairs and exited into the open room where the cargo hold was. Horses were to her right, and to her left was the engine room. The heart of Ulysses kept them afloat, and her heart and mind were also there as Gareth ran through her mind and body repeatedly since he left his room the morning before. She needed to talk with the man and was hesitant to do so.

The door was hot to the touch. She took a deep breath as she opened it, and the steam pushed the hair from her eyes as she stepped into the room. She pulled her hand to her mouth; it was not the smell but as if the room pulled the air from her very lungs as she entered.

Breathing wasn't the hardest thing to do in the room; she could hardly see anything in front of her for the steam. Mia could feel her clothing as it started to melt to her skin with sticky sweat. Her hand reached in front of her to be sure she did not walk into anything or anyone. "Hello," she called out; she knew nothing of the layout of the room. Two steps, and she stopped; her heart pounded through her chest, and she thought she could almost hear it over the sound of the steam engine churning. "Hello," she called out again a little louder, or at least she thought it was louder. Everything seemed to echo and muffle in her head.

Mia never felt him but knew he was there; quickly, she turned to look at his sweat-covered bare chest as he stepped up to her. A low, rumbling growl was different and close as she looked up at Gareth's muscular chin, sweat-covered face, and hair clung to his skin. He smiled; she still never knew how the man got behind her when she was only a few steps into the room.

"Miss me," he questioned in a low, gravelly voice, leaning forward, wrapping his hands on her upper legs and picking her up. The dress stopped her from wrapping her legs around his body, but she tried as she felt him wisp her off the floor a few steps away before he sat her down on a high-standing table. The table was tall enough that they were now eye to eye. She grinned, hands still on his hard shoulders and visions of the night before flashing in her mind. She blushed from the memories. It was as if he was built into the shadow, his mountain of a frame as steam and smoke surrounded them.

"This isn't the place," she stated, staring into his eyes as she pushed her hands forward until they met on the other side of his neck and her petite fingers intertwined into one another.

"Then why did you come down here in this *hot* place," he questioned as he stepped forward, his large hands on her knees, pushing them further open. Why did she come down here? This was not where she meant to go, but once she stood by the door, she could not stop. Her mind screamed at her not to come down here, but here she sat. This was not the place, but she wanted it even more than the first time. Still too many unanswered questions about the man now pushing her legs further open, wider; he was only moments from lifting her dress. She was wet, and it wasn't due to the sweat from the steam engine she could hear rattling in the background, even though her heart pounded louder in her mind.

She leaned forward until their lips met; Salvia hung to each as she slowly pulled away. She felt her dress pull from her legs as his hands met bare skin just above her leg. "We can't, not here... Stone."

"Likely fast asleep in his room. It'll be hours before he comes back to relieve me, and he is not who I want to think about." He grinned as he slowly moved forward, his lips on her neck. He could feel his tongue run against the softness of her skin. Every muscle in her body screamed out from his touch.

Outreaching arms, she pushed him back. "No." She smiled, having to look away from his eyes. "I don't know…"

"You don't know why you came down here." He grinned so big she thought she could count his teeth.

A deep breath and a large smile of her own, "I do…. I don't remember." She hesitated, and it was honest. She was still feeling guilty for the night before, but she found herself once again in his arms, hands on bare skin, and she wanted it again. "I need to go." She jumped to the floor, not realizing how far she was from the solid surface, but he caught her and sat her down softly on the floor, still with the boyish smile.

"I am sure we will pick this conversation up again," she still held her hands against his hard stomach, staring into his eyes in a haze of confusion. The man mesmerized her and drove her to lustful thoughts, almost making her forget about everything else. Sophia, and Kent Hardy, who was he? Julian's sickness, the fact he was still alive, meant he may pull through despite his thoughts.

"We will talk." She pushed up on her tiptoes to kiss his lips again, but he pulled away with a grin. Moving from her path, she knew the way out. As she exited the door, she stood at the other end of the closed wooden structure. She could almost feel his warm breath on the back of her neck as she was sure he was just on the other side.

She twisted her head to one side, looking back at the handle as she took a deep breath. Now was the time, the time to confront Hardy. What was Julian talking about?

Chapter Seventeen

Mia stepped through the door. She smiled at the little girl at the foot of the bed when she looked up at her from the journal the girl was writing in. It was curious. She had always noticed the girl reading. Seeing her tiny hands writing in the journal was another thing. She wondered what secrets the journal held. Mia never looked at Hardy, who sat on the bed with his hat pulled down on his eyes. It may have looked like he wasn't paying attention, but she noticed the twitch of his hand near the pistol when she entered. Mia knelt beside the little girl and, as she did so often, ran her hand across her forehead, pushing strands of red hair behind her ear. "How are you doing today, wildflower?"

The girl shut her journal before Mia could even peek to see what she was writing. They shared a smile before Mia stood, turned, and walked to the door, where she shut it. "Have you taken Sophia up to the viewing deck today?" Mia questioned. She needed to get Hardy alone but, at the same time, needed to be someplace where they could keep an eye on Sophia. Hardy pushed the hat up off his eyes and looked at her, an awkward smile as if the two spoke without saying a word. "No," he replied, shifting his feet off the bed. She had not even noticed the man was not wearing his boots. He took a moment, pulling them onto his feet before walking to the edge of the bed. Sophia was already standing. There was excitement on the child's face as she took Hardy's hand. The three of them ventured up to the viewing deck. As they exited the stairwell, Mia lowered to look at Sophia.

"Enjoy your book over here, far from the edge, okay?" Sophia smiled in reply before she walked away around the wall where she sat. Neither of the two moved until the little girl was once again deep in thought, writing in her journal. Mia led the way to the railing, where she leaned. It was not long since she had stood in the very spot with Julian the morning before. At least, she had thought only a brief time had passed as the light had grown dim with the sun setting someplace behind them. The light on the approaching Rocky Mountains had grown hazy, but the peaks themselves had grown large since she was last here.

Hardy leaned with his back to the railing. He kept a watchful eye on the little girl. "What is it, Mia? You look… confused about something."

"I have too many questions and too few answers. And to add to all, a conversation with Julian has left me with another, and I think you can answer it," Mia questioned.

"I don't know what you mean," he replied.

"I think you do, and you're going to tell me," she turned, leaning against the railing, looking back at Sophia. "For that little girl, you are going to tell me who the hell you are?" Hardy watched Sophia sympathetically and lovingly, in a way that only a family member could look over a child. "What is your secret, Kent Hardy? What aren't you telling me?"

Kent smiled, glancing at her and then back to Sophia before he turned, looking out into the birth of the coming dusk. A seriousness overtook his face like none she had seen on the man, and she always thought him to be serious. "Kent Hardy is dead."

There was a long pause; Mia looked at the man, confused about what she had just heard. "Then who are you?" A tight grip on the axe as it slides down her palm, like so many times, coming to a stop at a familiar touch of leather.

"I buried Kent Hardy myself, gun downed by a drunk, the very man whose life I count as the first I ever took," he stated with a sorrow-filled look. "I shot the man in the back twice, but still, he turned and shot at me. The truth is the first man I killed I shot three times, twice in the back like a common coward."

"Who are you? The little girl knows you… she is a trusting child, but I see how she looks at you and how you look at her… she told me she had a secret, and you are it."

"Kent Hardy was my cousin," he stated, lowering his head. "It is easy to take a man's identity when the two of you looked like brothers from the time you were both old enough to play in the dirt and mud together, two different upbringings, the same family, one a gunslinger. The other was a businessman in love with money and exploration, and new adventures… only by the time we were teenagers did we no longer look like." He glanced at Mia, and she knew the answer he was about to give: "I am Daniel Hope."

She again looked to Sophia, a smile on the little girl's face as if she knew she no longer had to keep her secret. "How is this… how did the others not know?"

"Not hard to change one's name when you don't look like the same person you were when last they saw you," Daniel stated. There was an odd smile in his expression. He was also glad to have the secret out in the open with someone. "I was a fat man, fat on money and wealth, yes. But I was probably 275 pounds when I disappeared from Washington, with someone wanting to frame me for a man's murder and no way to prove them wrong. I feared for my own life, for the life of my family." Mia looked over the thin, muscular man and was hard-pressed to see him that heavy when she was sure he was a mere 170 at most now. "Shaggy, almost shoulder-length hair and a beard since the time I could grow a full beard," Mia watched the man lift his hat and hold it tight in his hands, his hair cut short almost to the scalp with only the hint of a shadow on his face. Everything he was saying was hard to picture on the man standing before her. "It was easy to come back to Washington and stand in the room with men I once called friends, but they never even knew it was me. The hat pulled close to my eyes, the only feature I feared anyone could even recognize on me. Even my clothing, gone was my elegant gentlemen's attire… now the dusters of men of the west. Men of wealth and intelligence so often avoid looking another in the eyes when they consider them lesser men, made my deception so easy." Hardy smiled, putting his hat back on, Mia just stood and stared at the man. How could she not have seen this before, the way Sophia looked at him? The way she seemed to trust him. The secret she had been keeping all this time.

"And Julian, how did he know?" Mia questioned.

"The man is dying, or at least thinks so," Daniel stated. "We were never close, Julian and I; he was too strict and straight military. Not sure if he ever approved of me marrying his sister." There was a difference in his voice now, one of relief now that his secret was out. And it sounded softer to Mia as she listened. "Sophia wanted to see her uncle, knowing he was sick, and I took her to him. The man sat up the moment we entered the room and shut the door, lucid as you and I are speaking now and called me Daniel. It sent chills down my back; he did not even have to look into my eyes. He knew it was me where he didn't before. I am terribly sorry for the deception. I trusted you. I had heard stories about it from others… I trusted you… I have to ask… was it Frost?"

Mia smiled, looking down. "Do you believe the Frost family would put a hit on you or your daughter?" she questioned. It was a deflection as she had to run it through her mind without blurting out the desired answer. They both wanted it to be.

"I believe the Frost family may be behind a lot of what has happened the past few years… including the disappearance of your husband and others." Wide-eyed, open-mouthed, Mia turned to face him with her full body.

"You knew my Logan," she quickly questioned.

"I met him once, four years ago," Daniel replied. "We spoke for a small bit about his young wife."

"Where did he go?" she questioned. There was pressure in her eyes, and she could feel the tears, wanting to escape from the very mention of him.

"I only know whispers… he and a group of men and women set out for someplace in the Northwest... and sadly, even that could be a rumor. I do know it as for Hamilton, and he wanted to send for you the moment they were settled wherever it was they were going. From the day they left Washington, I truly don't know." Daniel reached forward and wiped the only tear to escape Mia's eye before she turned to look back out into the now darkness.

"I want to say yes, it was Frost," she quickly started to change the subject from Logan. "But nothing besides my hatred for the young man pushes the judgment. My mind is clouded. If not him, it was not Julian either."

"Nor Beck, I trusted his father, and despite the rumors of me being responsible, he would never pursue vengeance on a little girl," Daniel quickly stated.

"Smith is locked away, will be no threat to anyone for some time," Mia stated. "Same with Owens."

"And that leaves only Stone and…" There was a long pause.

"Gareth," Mia lowered her head, saying it out loud, almost breaking her heart, thinking it could be Gareth.

"The two of you have grown close… or is it purely physical?" Daniel questioned.

Mia paused, her mouth wide for a moment before she spoke, "I don't know what we are. But I don't believe he is the one."

"Could still be Frost, possibly," Daniel stated. Mia replied with a half-smile. At least some questions had been answered. They would set down in Colorado sometime early in the morning. A small group would ride out to get food supplies, and they would be on their way again. Less than three days until they would set down.

Chapter Eighteen

She woke when she felt Ulysses fall. The weight of the room seemed to shift as the vessel was going downward suddenly. Mia sat up, pushing the small sheet off her body. She could not remember when she went to bed, only the conversation with Daniel Hope. A secret she would now have to keep as well.

Mia quickly got off the bed. She had prepared her clothes for the day the night before. She pulled the thin leather dress top over her head, letting it rest on her body, bare shoulders, and arms except for a one-inch strap holding the top on her thin frame. Pulling a pair of tan pants from the suitcase. It had been far too long since she wore something other than cumbersome dresses. She pulled them up, her legs latching around her hips. Next were the moccasins, a vastly different material. They had thin soles with a padded bottom made for moving softly on hard ground, with reddish fur thick from just above the ankle to the very top of the boot resting just below her knee. It made an extra layer of warmth.

Pulling the leather band from the same position as the rest, she pulled it up, her arm resting on her bicep where she tied it tight, letting the long leather strands hand free. She placed the leather strap necklace around her neck, letting the little white feather hang freely around her neck. A three-inch-wide leather brown belt, she pulled it around her hips and latched it tightly. A small pouch attached to the belt was made to hold the pistol.

Mia moved to the small wash area, where she looked at her reflection in the mirror. It was a more natural look to her. One she had not seen in many years. It was Jean who got her the clothing shortly after Logan's disappearance. She smiled as she pulled the container free from the cabinet. She took her time to fix the faux hawk, something she hadn't done since the fight with Frost. When she finished, she applied the dark paint across the full width of her face, both above and below her eyes.

One last item to her wardrobe, she pulled the cloak from the suitcase, it was on the main bottom. Clad in leather and fur, she wrapped it around her shoulders and clasped it tight at the base of her neck as it hugged and warmed her body. She could not wear it for long inside the Ulysses, but she did not plan on staying inside long. She pushed the axe between the belt and pants. She felt the soft, sudden stop of the Ulysses; she knew they had touched down. She would not be accompanying the others to town; she needed time to clear her thoughts about everything.

The horse moved slowly through the thick snow, and Mia knew which way the others went. The road was evident that there had been some travelers here recently. A town rested a short few miles away. Gareth and Stone took the wagon to get enough food and other essentials to get through two to three more days of travel. She did little to push the horse, just a tug and twist here and there as they circled past the Ulysses. The heat from the ship melted the snow around her.

Mia came to a frozen stream and tied the horse off as she walked for a moment, stopping at the edge. She could hear the horse as it fidgeted and was aggravated at being alone in a strange place. The horse watched her as steam escaped its nostrils with each warm breath. The snow-covered ground and trees as the white hung to every surface.

Mia stepped on the edge of the ice. She could feel the chill as it generated from the ice and sent chills up her entire body. Several steps over the ice, she watched her feet. The horse got louder and louder, kicking and rumbling in its place. It was afraid of something, but still, it watched her. Turning, looking at the ice, the low rumbling growl sent a chill of fear and excitement up her back. Her hand was on her axe.

She never saw it. Only the feeling she was being watched, her skin began to crawl, axe free and in her familiar grasp in her right hand. Her left hand pulled the pistol free, and the growl remained distant. The small snow-covered embankment ahead, with its large dead tree looming over the water. It could have been mistaken for wind picking snow off the ground. It was so subtle, the breath from the wolf as it snarled, peeking its head around the tree. She took a breath of relief as she stepped back, till planted on the ice-covered water.

The animal moved more into sight; its white belly blended into the snow with matted fur. Its thick gray coat and red highlight mixed with the dark gray. The animal's head was low to the ground, but its eyes never moved from her, and the weight of nearly one hundred and twenty-five was almost the same size as hers. Its lips curled and snarled as it showed its blood-soaked teeth. The animal had a fresh kill somewhere nearby. Likely alone coming to investigate an intruder in its territory. She smiled; this animal did not mean her harm, just protecting a meal. It continued to approach, snarling as it stepped to the edge of the water. Mia could feel her heart pound with excitement. With a tight grip on her weapons, she stepped side, watching it close, ignoring the panicked sound of the horse behind her.

The sound of a branch being moved broke her gaze on the wolf to her left movement. The twitch of her head, the large black wolf's lips as it watched her with ill intentions. Everything about the new wolf sent a chill of fear up her back, replacing the excitement, and there was no color change to the beast except the small white underbelly. Black as night from its nose to the tip of its long, full tail, the beast seemed more than twice the size of the other. This one was a threat. Mia turned to position her frame to face the new wolf, only keeping a pacing glance to the other as she stepped further out onto the ice. She felt the slick surface under her feet. If they wanted her, they would have to come out on it to get to her. The big black wolf stopped at the edge of the ice, just like the other watching her. Still, the beast licked its teeth, and unlike the other, there was no presence of blood. This one had not been eating. The wolf snapped its jaws, and the sound of them coming together made a loud crack. It wanted her to run. It craved a chase. One Mia would not give in to; her chances became less if she tried to run. She must face the animal and show it no fear, even though every muscle screamed for her to flee.

A long, deep breath as the steam from the hot hair floated across her face, "I don't want to hurt you." She muttered, still on the ice, and took a step toward the big black one. It snarled, taking a step backward. A glance at the gray as it walked the edge of the ice circling behind her. She stepped further out onto the ice and toward the big black one. The howl of the gray sent chills as she glanced back at the beast with its head held high, perfect white fur matching the snow extended out for the bellowing sound. Mia gritted her teeth and continued to keep the gray in sight with the black.

She heard the first sound of nails on ice; the gray was coming two steps out, snarling. Teeth were easy to see. Mia stepped toward it and watched as it again backed off the ice. Then back to the black, two steps back to where she was before.

"GET," she yelled out two quick steps toward it. The black backed up into the snow, twisting its body and running around the edge away from her. The wolf never stopped until it was within a foot of the other. She could see the horse in the background still tied tightly to its tree but struggling to free itself, but the wolves did not care for the animal. They saw her as their quarry.

Mia screamed as loud as she could muster as she charged four steps toward the two beasts. The gray scattered, running the direction it had come and out of sight to protect its meal. The black waited, snarling at it, and took a couple of steps toward her. She paused; feet slid out from under her as she collapsed to the ice with a crash.

The wolf leaped from its back legs; with her left hand raised, she pulled the trigger. She heard the yelp of pain from the large beast as it landed near her but was no longer interested as it pawed at its neck.

Mia slides, pushing away from the wounded animal and the blood-covered ice. The wolf continued to paw and whine at its fresh wound as the bullet cut through the side of its flesh. Sliding to the edge, she dug into the snow, pushing her way back to her knees. The gray wolf reappeared, watching from a safe distance. She tucked the pistol back in its garter and stood holding the axe with both hands as she walked through the snow, keeping an eye on the gray now more than the black.

Two steps from the ice now back to the small path she had used to step to the ice, the gray looked at her and began to growl again. "Go, return to your meal." The wolf twisted its head as if it understood what she said. To one knee, she dug into the deep snow until she felt the hard presence and pulled the rock free. A quick throw, hitting the wolf on its bounce, but no real reaction besides the flinch of its back legs from the hit. "I mean no harm," she called out.

The black wolf walked to the edge and just as quickly ran off into the wilderness, the gray wolf not far behind. Mia quickly moved to the horse; the animal had calmed almost from the moment the wolves were gone. Quickly, she untied it, mounted it, and headed back toward the Ulysses.

The horse panted, and the steam from its breath smacked Mia in the face as they traveled down the trail. Fresh snow was beginning to fly; the cloak was tightly against her, and she could feel the pinch of the axe on the belt. A position she was not used to holding the weapon in. She leaned forward; she could feel the thump of the horse's heart, and the animal was still tensed. "Shh," she tried to calm the beast. "They are gone." The large horse began to trot, picking its hooves way off the ground out of the snow as they moved forward.

The black wolf came from her right, leaping toward her and the horse. The horse lifted onto its hind legs. Teeth struck skin; its large jaw dug into the soft flesh of the horse's neck. The horse shook, trying to get away from the beast.

Mia landed on her back, stunned, and for a moment, she did not know what had happened. The snow hugged her as she sat up just to see her horse fall to the ground. The wolf looked over its new kill, but the kill was not important. It had a taste for revenge and the victim in its eyes. Snarled, snowing its blood-soaked teeth on Mia as it circled the dead mass of the horse. Mia thought about the pistol, which was still empty as she did not take time to reload. The neck of the wolf was matted with its blood from Mia's shot. Slowly, leg after leg, it approached her. She sat in the snow with a clear look at its hate-filled yellow eyes. The axe in her left hand was not her strongest arm for an attack, but it would have to do. She waited, but the wolf did not. It leaped again. Blade smashed into a skull. Mia put all her weight into pushing her way from the ground and crashing her weapon into its head. Face-first in the blood-soaked snow, she glanced up. The beast still twitched but was dead. Her weapon cleaved into its skull.

Mia glanced back to the horse. It no longer moved. Back to the wolf, and she saw the breath of the gray as it sat glaring at her. Head twisted, and mouth closed, it looked into her eyes. The adrenaline was not there. Too cold and in shock from the attack, Mia found it hard to breathe, let alone get ready for another attack. When her weapon was still in the head of the other several feet away. It approached slowly and stopped at the head of the black. Nose to its fur, it leaned back, and its chest grew as it howled. Three times, each time sent a chill down Mia's already numb back. When the third verse was done, the beast howled and ran away.

Chapter Nineteen

Mia woke, startled to find herself in her bed on board the Ulysses. She pushed the covers off, and she saw her axe cleaning and sitting on the small dresser just inside the room. As well as the clothing she was wearing before, she shifted her legs off the bed. She quickly walked across the room, lifting the clothing, which was clean and fresh. The smell of jasmine, one she could not resist. She lifted the shirt and quickly pulled it over her head. The smell was refreshing. She took a deep breath, holding the neck to her nose, and smiled. The last thing she remembered was the gray wolf leaving… how did she get here?

Mia pushed her feet into the dry moccasins, putting nothing else on, and rushed out into the hall. There was something different about the Ulysses now. The shaking of the great vessel was more evident as if it had lost course. Much like a boat of the sea on rough waters, she felt something was wrong. She rushed to Hardy's room and immediately saw the blood. The bed sheets were soaked, not a dry stitch among the once-white linens. "SOPHIA," she yelled, rushing to the bed. There was nobody. She went out into the hall again and back to her room, but the moment she went to enter, she was stopped. The door would not budge. Repeatedly, she thrust her shoulder into the wooden structure, but it would not move.

"Sophia," she whispered, "I am sorry." How could she have failed? But where was everyone else?

She rushed to the mess hall, sliding to a stop the moment she saw the table. Much like the girl's bed, covered in blood. So much blood… Too much blood in the two spots to have all come from one little girl. Her heart pounded. She rushed past the table and never stopped, skipping multiple steps at a time until she emerged out into the hall. Into the captain's chamber, more blood. How was this possible? She walked to the viewing glass just beyond the chair and saw the dark skies ahead? The Ulysses was traveling through a storm, and lightning struck out just in front of the vessel. Where was Beck?

Out of the room, she rushed. Julian's room was locked. She pounded on the door, "Julian… are you in there?" She continued to pound at the door when she heard a crash of thunder. Even over the muffled sound in the halls, she heard it. Five more times, she pounded at the door, each louder than the one before. Down the hallway and another set of stairs, she rushed. The cargo holds more blood, a lot more, all the signs of slaughter, but by whom. In each room, she searched, every cell she did not stop until she was again rushing through the mess hall, having found no one. Again, she pushed on her door, and still, it did not move. There was still one last place she had not looked. Out of the stairway, she rushed. She looked out into the flashes of light. Lightning strike after strike as it lit up the dark sky.

Mia watched, mesmerized at the storm, stuck now walking forward. At first, she didn't see him standing at the railing. She stopped the moment she knew she was being watched; the feeling crept up her skin. His eyes were on her as she turned, and at first, she did not recognize him. Did the crew pick up someone new when they went for supplies? "Hello," she said out loud.

"Meghana," the man called out. The voice cut through her. "Don't you recognize me?"

Mia did now, but how could she not? He was in her dreams, a man she hated at first but grew to love and even marry. She rushed to him, and quickly they hugged. She held tighter than she could hold a person. She knew then that this was all a dream. "Hold me,' she said softly.

"You failed, Mia," his voice echoed, but she did not move. "You slept with another; you failed me." She opened her eyes and even stopped breathing for a moment. "He is here."

"Mia," she turned, Gareth was there. Shirtless, he held his axe covered in blood. "He killed them, Mia."

Mia turned to look at Logan. "Logan?" He smiled when she said his name. She wanted to wake up now. He shoved her to the hard floor as he pulled his hand out from behind his back and the bloody knife.

"Was not I who killed them," Logan replied, but his smile told her otherwise.

"Mia," again Gareth's voice cut through her, but she looked to Logan, his eyes almost wolf life as he glared down at her. He flashed his teeth and his large canine. Gareth yelled her name again, "MIA."

"Don't you die on me...?" She felt herself being picked up from the ground. "Mia..." She felt Gareth's arms wrapped around her and knew everything was going to be okay, but she never lost sight of Logan. "...Mia."

• • •

Mia woke. The covers fell from her body as she sat up. She was covered in a cold sweat...she was again waking in her bed, not knowing how she got here. He sat in a chair, one which was not there before. His hulking frame leaned forward, looking over at her. "Mia..." Gareth whispered as if unsure of what he was seeing.

Mia felt her head. She was running at a feverish temperature. Shifting her legs over the edge of the bed, she could see her clothing bundled on the floor. Gareth was on his feet with a cup of water in hand, pushing it in front of her. "It is tea. Drink it…it will help with the fever." She took the glass from his hand. His other hand reached out, touching her forehead. His hand chilled to the touch, and she smiled. "You gave us quite the scare," he leaned down until he was positioned on his knee, looking at her as she sipped a small drink of the bitter tea.

"How did I get here," she questioned through the chatter of her teeth. She was burning up but freezing at the same time.

"We got back before you and waited an hour before Beck and I rode out. It was nearly dark when we found you… in the snow, you foolish girl. What were you thinking?" Gareth questioned as he knocked hair from her eyes.

"The w-wolf," she stuttered.

"Big black one, biggest I have ever seen. You did quite the number on him," Gareth stated. "Kept what we could figure you would want the hide for a new cloak. Your old one was pretty badly torn by a gray one… best we can figure, she dragged you nearly a quarter of a mile but never touched you."

Mia smiled; the gray wolf never wanted to do her harm, and she could see it in its eyes. The same lonesome look she could now see in Gareth. "How long was I out?" she questioned before she took another drink of the tea. Her face expressed her displeasure with the taste, and Gareth let lose a small laugh.

"Over a day." She looked over the glass at him, his big brown eyes staring back at her.

Her lips parted as she tried to ask a question, "…how long before we dock?"

"Twelve, maybe fourteen hours," Gareth stated. Mia saw her axe sitting in a position similar to that of her dream. "Was afraid you might not wake; the fever was a bad one. You were dreaming, before you woke, of your husband."

"And you…" she said before she took a sip of tea. "You were there as well." Gareth looked away but continued to smile; she reached forward, touching his chin. "Once we are docked in California… what you will do?" she questioned. She wanted an answer to a question she could not answer herself.

Mia glared into his eyes; she wanted an answer. Selfishly, it would add to her thoughts about what she was to do when she was free of Sophia as her ward. "I don't know," Gareth replied. He had taken a position on both of his knees in front of her. It was then she realized she was fully exposed to him naked with just a small sheet stretched across her lap, and she blushed. "I have an option of staying on with the Ulysses, but there are… other things I have to consider." He shyly smiled. Her blush continued, making her look even more flushed; he again placed a hand on her forehead. She sipped her tea with one hand, using her free to pull his hand away, and smiled.

"I will be all right," she said.

"I know what you're going through," he said with certainty.

"What do you mean?" Mia questioned.

"Your husband," he replied. "I was married once… a lifetime ago…" He stood away from the bed. Mia did not know what to say… "Beck is preparing a meal for everyone, some special recipe or an Elk Stone killed, and I have some mint soup for you to help with the fever," Gareth stated. "It is a few hours away; he wanted the meal to be closer to our touch down, the last meal of the maiden voyage. You should get some sleep." She took a last drink of the tea and set it on the bedside table. Gareth stood and started to walk away, but she quickly grabbed his wrist, holding him back. She still did not know what to say to his revelation. He softly kissed her on the forehead. "You need to get some sleep." He pulled at the cover as she shifted her legs back onto the bed. Gareth pulled the sheet up over her body. "I will be here when you wake." She smiled as he left the room.

Chapter Twenty

Three soft knocks, all in succession, followed again by three more after a momentary pause. Mia sat up. She had managed to pull a long shirt over and a thin dress but could do nothing about the dizziness. She had a problem steadying herself as she crossed the room. As she opened the door, the first thing she saw was Sophia, a book in her hand, as always. She reached out her hand, taking Mia in her tiny grasp. Mia lowered and ran a hand across the side of her face, pushing the red curls behind her ear. "The last dinner of the maiden voyage of the Ulysses," Daniel Hope stated as he leaned against the opposite wall. "She wants you to eat with her, and I think you should too."

"I am not feeling up to it," Mia stated, looking up at him and then back to Sophia, who smiled her sweet smile, a smile she could not resist even in her feverish state. "Okay," she whispered. She turned, took a glance at the room, her axe still on the table, and then went back to Hope. She would have no reason to be armed, not with him there.

Mia, with Sophia still holding her tight grip, walked out into the hall, and the three of them went to the mess hall. Mia was surprised to see Julian there. With his bronze mask on his face, he sat straight and watched the three of them as they entered. She had not even thought about asking about the man since she woke, but seeing him now, he looked almost better. Stone sat at his left; he looked at the table, his large arms positioned in front of him as his chin rested. He never so much as looked at them as they entered.

Daniel sat in the third seat from the end, and Sophia let loose of Mia's hand for the first time and took the seat beside him. Mia approached the last chair at the table and leaned against it just as Gareth entered the room. He had two bowls in his hand, setting the first in front of Julian. He smiled when he saw Mia approach and set the second in front of where she was to be sitting. "I thought I would have to drag you from the bed," Gareth stated with a grin, one she repeated just with a weaker structure.

"No such chance this time," she replied. She could smell the soup and watched the steam rise from it. Gareth took a seat across from her. It was then Beck entered the room. She had not smelled it before, but the smell of fried steak floated and hung to every corner of the room. He set the large tray in the center of the table and pulled the cover free to expose the food, steaks, and potatoes, and the steam floated from the center all around the table. The smell made her mouth water.

"The maiden voyage of the Ulysses," Beck said with a smile, taking a seat beside Stone.

"It may not have been ideal," Julian proclaimed as he stood. He used the table to sturdy himself. "But in a matter of hours, we will land, and it will be declared a success." Gareth and Stone began to pound on the table in celebration. Followed by Beck, Daniel, and even Sophia with a big grin of excitement. Only Mia and Julian did not. Beck walked to a small counter and pulled out a bottle. "Hamilton sent this along for the last dinner, and he wanted us to have a special drink." There were large goblets set out in front of each of them. He went around pouring each cup full, even Sophia's, and he left only a small amount for the child. Stone almost looked lost as he started to place steaks and potatoes on each plate and spread them around until each had their own. He stopped just behind Gareth and looked at the others. But especially to Mia and then Sophia, "Are you excited to see your mother, child?" he questioned with a big grin. It was the first time he had smiled since they entered the room. And it was then Mia saw the look in his eyes, the same look the black wolf had given her. Her heart almost stopped; it was never Frost. She glared at Stone, having for a moment forgotten she had left her weapon behind in her room. But she still had no proof… it could have been her fever making her delusional.

Mia sat back in her chair; it was as if all the wind had knocked from her body, and she couldn't retrieve it. Her mouth wide, she stared at Stone, whose eyes met hers, and he smiled. Her hand twitched on the table, but only a spoon sat in front of her. She felt Sophia's hand on her other hand, and she broke her starring instantly to look at the girl. How could he want to kill her? What reason could he have? She was in shock. She had no proof, already killed one man on the journey… Broken another's wrist… She would have to wait.

"Are you okay?" Gareth questioned.

Mia took a deep breath. "Yes…" She paused as she looked to Stone, who was now taking his seat back at the other end of the table. "Everything is just fine…" She felt it as if her blood began to boil. This was no fever dream or delusion; she was sure of it, and her eyes were now bloodshot with anger.

"I would like to say grace before everyone digs in." Julian seated as Beck stood to speak, though everyone had a plate of food and wine in front of them. It was as if each of them waited for someone else to start the last meal of the first journey of the astonishing Ulysses. "Bless us, Father, it has been a long time coming. In a matter of hours, we will land at our destination, and for some, we will be reunited with loved ones. And for others, it is just the beginning of our lives; a new world is in front of us. Bless Julian, who seems to have recovered from the poison. Bless Mia, who gave us all a fright. She is just as lucky to be with us today." '*Unlucky for Stone*," the words were on her tongue, and she could taste them. Wanting to say them aloud, she stared at the man; sweat began to bubble on her head. Her skin crawled just underneath a scratch, an itch she wanted to stop. She wanted to say something. The wolf's eyes were the same. She had not even realized Beck was still talking; the roar of her voice in her head blocked it. "Amen," she crashed back to reality as the last word was said.

Mia looked down at Sophia, who still held her hand but stared forward. Mia looked over at Daniel Hope. She wanted to tell him, but how would he react? When she was still not fully sure herself, he would shoot him dead the moment the words left her lips. Kent Hardy would shoot the man dead in an instant, no questions asked. And though she knew the truth, he was not Hardy; the man sitting there was no longer Daniel Hope either.

Julian Bastion, Stone was arms reach away, tearing into his steak. How would Julian act if he knew the man next to him was going to try to kill his sister's daughter? He would take the knife, now in his hand, and slice his throat.

She stared across the table at Gareth; she wasn't the only one not eating. His jaw twisted in preparation to speak, but no words escaped his lips. His eyes were dark and squinted as he watched her. He leaned on the table. It would have been easy to reach across and kiss the man, now in front of everyone. And whisper in his ear, telling him Stone was a threat to the little girl and Mia. How would he react? Would he believe her? She would hope the moment he heard the whisper, he would slowly cross the room, taking his massive arms… and snap his neck. So many ways to kill the man. She felt almost everyone there would do it for her; all she had to do was speak.

Her lips parted; just as he looked up, goblet in hand, he took a drink and stared into her eyes. He raised his cup in the form of toast and a smile. Her petite fingers were on the thick glass, and she lifted it in reply and took a drink of the sweet wine as well. She smiled. She could tell no one. She may have been positive it was him, but she knew what had to be done. She was hired to protect Sophia Hope, and she would do just that. And she would kill Stone. She would just have to wait for him to make his move; it would not be long.

After dinner, Mia pulled Daniel to the side just outside her room. "I need you to take Sophia to Julian's room and stay there until Ulysses lands," she had hoped he would not ask questions. Daniel pulled his second gun, holding it out to her. "Thank you," she replied. "But I don't need it."

"Please be safe," Daniel replied, taking Sophia by her hand. Mia didn't move until both were gone from sight. She entered her room, taking a deep breath. It wouldn't be long. She put Logan's vest on, followed closely by her axe. She never heard the door open, but she did not jump when she felt his hands on her hips, his warm breath on the back of her neck. An out reached the arm over her forehead.

"You are still running a fever." He pulled her back against him.

"It is passing, though." She could feel his heart beating against her back, and her pulse raced as his grip got tighter.

"Beck said we will be landing in less than two hours. I wish I could stay here and watch us land with you in my arms."

"But you must help Stone," she said with a smirk.

"At dinner… what was that? Is there something you want to tell me about Stone?" Gareth questioned. "Or was it about what I said?"

She twisted until she faced him. "It is nothing you need to worry about."

"You are lying," Gareth said with a smile.

"Maybe," she quickly shot back with a smile and a kiss to his lips.   "After we land… we have a lot to discuss."

"Yes, we do," he replied, giving her another kiss before releasing his grip and heading off for their landing preparations.

"Meghana, my birth name is Meghana." He smiled before disappearing.

Chapter Twenty-One

Mia remembered another time in her life. Sometimes, it seemed so long ago that it was a dream. She fought an older boy in her tribe. She had humiliated him in front of not only the other children but the adults of the tribe. Including her father. She thought she was to be scalded or punished for such a thing, but her father had taken her to see a shaman. She remembered that night now as if it was the day before. Minutes felt like hours. Mia felt each heartbeat, wishing Ulysses had already landed. Her assignment was almost over, and yet, no one had even attempted to take the little girl's life. But she knew… he was coming. She could still see the wolf's eyes each time she shut her own. She sat on the bed, legs crossed under her with her palms resting on her knees, much the same way she had sat that night with the shaman. His boots softly traveled down the hall; each footstep might as well have been that of two dozen soldiers thundering toward her. It all sounded the same in her meditation. The door crept open, his face shadowed and dark, but there was no mistaking who it was. His body engulfed and blocked most of the light from escaping into the dark room.

Rodney Stone smiled; it was the same smile she had seen him give Sophia so many times at the dinner table. It was all she could see, the large smile as the shadows engulfed the rest of his face as if he wore a demonic mask. "Where is she?"

"Some place safe," Mia replied. Her hands tightened into fists, and she started to sweat, feeling the cool touch of warm air on the back of her neck. *It's him. How could you not know it was him all this time?*

"How did you know?" Stone ran a hand over his thick beard with his left hand, and a large knife was shown in his exposed right hand, sitting with ease on his hip. He intended to do it up close, having to look the little girl in the eyes as he killed her. "We don't have to do this. Just tell me where you have hidden her, and I'll make it look like you tried. A few bruises, no one could blame you. You're just a **woman**." He bit his lower lip, leaving a snide tone in the last word.

Mia gritted her teeth so tightly she felt as if they'd break. "I never truly knew, not until now. To be honest, part of me still thought it may have been Frost. I so wish it had been him. You asked her if she was excited to see her mother, and I realized you had never said so much as a word to the girl. You only smiled at her. And spoke to others about her but never directly to Sophia."

"As easy as that?" Stone stated, looking away from her, his face filled with disappointment, and the knife began to bounce on his leg, showing his frustration with his tale.

"I must ask, why?" Mia asked, he looked back at her and grinned the sinister shadow mask once again on his face, and she remembered something shaman had said all those years before. *'Protecting a young girl from a demon.'* The old man's smooth voice seemed to reflect as Stone took a step toward her.

"Money, of course," he replied with a hollow laugh, his face still hidden in the shadow.

"Yeah, as simple as that you would kill a little girl for money. I suppose it would be a waste of time to ask who was paying?" she replied, but she still did not move from the bed. Or her meditation position. Stone only smiled.

"Never thought it was Gareth?" he questioned. "A pity I killed the brute for nothing, thinking he would get the credit for her death and I would be the hero."

Mia's heart stopped as she flushed with anger, moving her leg back in his direction, and the man laughed. "He may not be dead; I mean, he could survive the wound I gave him if you go now. Just tell me where the girl is, and I will trade you, his life, for the girl's." The man waved his knife around and continued to smile. "Meghana" was possibly the last word she told both the men in her life. She had known Gareth for a very short time, but he filled a part of her she had been missing.

Mia stood, lifting her hand in the air. Stone's eyes grew. It was the first time he saw the pistol. She pulled the trigger and seemed to move in slow motion as Stone fell back into the hall and out of sight. She could see the blood splatter on the wall behind where he had been standing. She rushed to the door, and almost immediately, she ran into his backhand, knocking her to the floor. She held at her lip; she could taste the blood. Her blood, he had split her lip in one hit. She was sure there would be a lot of pain to come, but she was shocked and numb from the hit. He stood over her, hand on the side of his neck; she could see the blood seeping through his fat fingers, maybe she wasn't as good of a shot as she'd thought. "Bitch," he muttered, pulling his hand away only to take a glance. She could see the bullet had just grazed his neck, she'd been aiming for his forehead.

Mia turned and began to crawl away. She was several feet into her crawl, trying to retrieve the axe from her vest, and realized it was not there. No axe and no pistol. She turned, sitting on the floor; it was the first thing she saw, her weapon of choice in his free fat hand. "I just had a marvelous idea, you Indian bitch," he said, grinning. He never moved from where he had been standing when he struck her. "You almost made this too easy," he glared at the weapon for a moment before he pushed it into his belt. She knew exactly what he was planning; he was going to kill Sophia with her weapon. If he made it past Daniel Hope was a different story. It allowed her not to think about the little girl she had been asked to protect. Her father would do as much. Gareth, though, was there in her mind, her last word to him, her name… the night they spent together. This could not be the end of them. She had to be with him again. She turned to stumble forward until she was to her feet and the door leading up the stairs to the viewing deck. She couldn't fight Stone, not here. The man was too big and physical, and she was unarmed. She needed someplace to maneuver. The same place where she had fought Frost was her best option.

She felt him. The moment she started up the stairs, his laugh echoed through the narrow hallways. Stumbling several times, step by step, she climbed. She could hear the pounding of his boots several steps behind her, casually following. Not even trying to keep up with her. She felt winded, finally reaching the door, and fell to her hands and knees as she opened it. She crawled. Her face hurt; she spat blood from her mouth as she could taste it building in the back of her throat. Two steps forward, she felt him, his hand in her hair, taking her to her feet. He shoved her back to the floor, sliding away, and again he laughed.

"I have been watching you, Indian, day after day, as you watched me and everyone on this ship," Stone said, leaning down beside her just as Mia pushed herself from the floor to her knees. Another backhand slapped across her face, the left side of her face the same side Frost had cut. "You are supposed to be this unstoppable killing machine, but I have been watching, and you know what I saw?" She had fallen to her back, legs tucked under her. She rose onto her elbows and started to roll over. She screamed out in pain as the three-hundred-pound man placed his boot on her wrist and let his weight settle. She clawed and smacked at his foot until he released her, but not due to her actions. He walked around to her head and leaned down again. "This is no fun if you do not at least try or give any witty comebacks… it is almost boring." Again, he grabbed a handful of hair, dragging her toward the railing as she kicked, screamed, and clawed at his hands the fifteen-foot walk. He never slowed until he reached the railing. He released and looked at the loose strands of black hair in his hand and blew them into the wind.

His thick-fingered hand was around her throat as he leaned down, inches from her face. "Do you know what I saw, squaw?" he whispered so low she almost didn't hear him because of the ringing in her head. "I saw a woman. A simple, housebroken savage who was no more a threat to me and my task than some wet nurse, I am almost disappointed." Stone stood looking out into the approaching landscape and smiled, casually taking in what he was seeing. "Truly is a lovely vision, is it not?" he questioned, turning and looking back at her. Again, he lowered down and placed his hand around her neck and squeezed until she coughed, and then he released.

"Fight back, damn it," he said, taking a handful of hair and pulling her close enough. He kissed her. His beard rubbed her face for a moment before he pulled away, biting down on her lip. As he released, she spat blood into his face and smiled, busted lip and bloodied gums visible. "Disgusting bitch." Yet another backhand to her face, she rolled away from him on impact, once again crawling away.

"Where do you think you are going?" He walked forward.

He kicked his stubby legs, kicking her in the stomach and rolling her for a couple of turns away from him. Mia gasped and coughed, trying to catch her breath, but nothing came to her. "Think you are going to find someone to help you?" The man laughed and walked forward, cutting into the path she would take back to the door. "Gareth is dead, honey; you will not be riding that studhorse again. Gutted like a fish." His shoulder was soaked in blood from the bleeding wound on his neck. It showed no sign of slowing. "Or maybe Beck? Look at where we are, sweetheart. That slave has himself a new master. He only cares about the Ulysses, Captain Beck, he so proudly proclaimed himself. Guess how disappointed he is now that the old man may pull through. I could take you to Smith, down in his cell. He would love to have some one-on-one time with you. He would love to break you down like some cheap dime store whore for what you did to him. Which I can't blame him, a tasty treat I am sure you were before the brute Gareth had you." The man circled to Mia's legs, grabbing her by the ankle and pulling her toward the center of the viewing deck. She still struggled to catch her breath from the kick to her stomach.

"You… will… not… break me…" She coughed, trying to turn and claw at the wood, but he continued to drag until he was satisfied with his destination.

"So, she speaks," he said with a laugh, staring down at her. "Again, my paw always said if it was wet, have at 'er, son. My father was a demented old bastard, but you know sometimes he was wise," Stone said. He ran a hand up the inside of her leg. She moved forward and dug her fingernails into his face, pulling down and cutting through the skin.

Stone twirled away from her, laughing as he did, "That is more like it," he called out. Mia reached her feet and stumbled away, only three hobbling steps before he was again on her, kicking her legs out from under her. "I am just getting started with you." She hit her head again on the hard floor and rolled over to her side in a fetal position.

Stone felt his face and the blood from the fresh claw marks and laughed, reaching down and taking both her ankles. "You are wrong, I will break you." The man pulled her closer.

He did not have as tight a grip as he intended. She pulled her left leg free, kicking upward, connecting with his face. He stumbled backward away from her but remained on his feet. He turned to look at her, no longer laughing as blood poured from his broken nose. Mia pushed up into a sitting position and then slowly moved to her feet. She felt the tug of clothing and then the indescribable feeling of a knife running through her skin. Her side as he cut just below the ribcage. She leaned forward, attempting to move away, but he held a tight grip, ripping at her vest.

Stone was not going to let her go. She lunged into him, biting and ripping with the only weapon she had. Now, it was not her blood dripping from her mouth as she spat the bottom of his ear to the floor. The man pushed her away, now rolling away. Mia laughed. A hollow echo of a laugh as she sat on her knees, wiping the blood from her chin.

She looked around and saw the axe still in his belt. Slowly, she stood. Almost the moment Mia was at her feet, he was again to his. He looked for a moment at the piece of his ear there on the floor, his blood-soaked hand then to the woman responsible. "You dare laugh?" Mia only smiled as she ran her arm across her chin again.

Stone walked toward her; she was close enough to hit his chin with a closed fist. Stone shied away from the impact, glanced back, and watched as Mia took a couple of steps back from him. Closer to the door, she crept, keeping an eye on him. The man charged, tackling her to the ground and again crashing his weight down on her and knocking her breath out. She wheezed, rolling over to her stomach, and started to push from the floor. Again, the man kicked her, this time in the left shoulder, rolling her several turns away. "T-This is over," he stuttered, looking for his knife, never realizing he had dropped it near the railing.

Mia raced to the door as fast as she could in her weakened state. She heard the man cuss from behind her. She leaned to the wall, leaping steps, hoping to keep her footing.

Out into the half, she heard him thundering down the stairs behind her. She didn't have much time. She had to be quick. She staggered through her door, almost falling on her entrance, the suitcase on the floor still open. She pushed her hand into the clothes, finding her desired object and pulling it free. Back on her feet, she raced out into the hall only to be greeted with yet another backhand from Stone. Bloodied, she crawled down the hall away from the large man. Her weapon and his knife in his hands, he laughed; she felt the deep cut on her side. Her face felt broken from the number of hits she had taken. She sat up on her knees and felt his hand on her shoulder.

"I promise to slit the little girl's throat quick and enjoy it much less than this." She turned fast, pulling the sharpened antler from the belt, and thrust it up. A trophy from a kill she had made with her husband and friends. Made into a weapon the night they made love, and it had a special place in her heart. She reached forward, pulling the axe from his hand, and smiled. Stone stared blankly from his one remaining eye. The laughing had stopped as he staggered backward away from her and fell to his back dead. She had stabbed the sharp point of the buck antler through the bottom of his chin, exiting his left eye.

Mia stumbled backward onto her back. She felt the shift of the Ulysses. They were close to landing. It was over.

"Gareth," she muttered his name. She sat up, standing careful not to put weight on her bruised shoulder. She gently pulled the vest off and let it lie on the floor. Lightly pulling her arm into her, it hurt to even move from where Stone had kicked her. Most of her body ached for one reason or another. She felt the cut on her side. She was afraid to look. Now, she only wanted to see if Gareth was alive.

Past the table in the mess hall to the stairs, she slowly walked, leaning against the wall with her good shoulder. She came to the next door, took a deep breath, and stepped out. Slowly, she walked to the engineer's room, and then she saw Sophia. Standing hand in hand with her father, she leaned against the door, almost unable to speak.

It was Beck who saw her, "What the hell happened?" He rushed to her side, helping her to a chair. He took his time to look over her wounds. Daniel Hope had pushed Sophia behind him to try to stop her from seeing the shape Mia was in.

"Stone," she muttered.

"Is he dead?" Hope questioned. Mia nodded her head yes, wondering where he and the girl were when Stone came looking for the child.

"Gareth, he said he killed Gareth…" Mia looked up. The bruise on her face was becoming more evident.

"We'll be on the ground in about twenty minutes…" Beck turned to look at Hope.

"I'll go check on Gareth," he stated as he turned to look at Sophia. "I want you to go sit in the captain's chair, and you listen to William, okay?" Sophia nodded, quickly following her father's instructions.

"You knew?" Mia questioned, looking at Beck, then to Hope. "You knew he was not Hardy?"

Beck turned to look at Hope as he walked past and out of sight to check on Gareth. "Not until about an hour ago," Beck said, glancing to Sophia and then to Mia. "We need to get you to a doctor first thing when we land."

"I will live," Mia said with a half-smile.

Beck moved back to the controls of the Ulysses as Mia left her place on the rear wall. She slid down. Her eyes shut as she felt some comfort on the solid surface. She felt the tug of another, and she opened her eyes. Sophia sat on her knees at her side, her tiny hand in Mia's own petite, bloodied grip.

"What will happen once we land?" Mia questioned; she wasn't even sure if she spoke the words as she glared at the back of Beck's head. It was all the man she could see.

"What do you mean?" he questioned.

"To the Ulysses, there must be some bigger plan…" Mia questioned. She heard the distinct laugh from Beck.

"Something you will have to take up with Julian now that he is back on his feet." Beck twisted to look back at her. It was the last thing she remembered before she blacked out.

Epilogue

Mia woke to the sound of hammering, walking, and people chattering all about. She rose in her place and looked around; she was nestled in her bed with large covers over her. There was a chill to the Ulysses she had never felt before. She shifted her legs off the bed and realized she was in a long, loose-fitting gown. She pulled the hoop dress up and quickly slipped into her moccasins before she walked to the door. She found it locked; she twisted the bolt and opened the door.

Immediately, she had to step to one side as a large woman walked past, giving her only a momentary glance. It was obvious to Mia they had landed while she was unconscious; she stepped back into the room. Quickly walking back to the small mirror in the offset of her room. The bruise on her face was purple and scarred. She took several deep breaths. Sophia. She had to see about the little girl. As she left the mirror, she saw the small envelope on the counter. She rushed to it and opened it and sifted through the money, more than she had ever seen at once. She came to a stop when she saw the small folded white paper, pulled it free, and opened it.

"Thank you. I can never thank you enough for what you did for our daughter and Daniel.

-   The Hopes"

She was released from her duties; Sophia was safe with her mother, and no doubt it came as a surprise to see her husband along with her. Mia wished she could have been there to see them reunited. She tucked the envelope into her suitcase, plucked the white feather necklace from the bedpost, and placed it around her neck.

Out the door, she raced. She wanted to see outside for herself first. She stepped out onto the viewing deck and was surprised to see Julian Bastion there. Leaning on a long cane, he never so much as smiled when he saw her. A glance back to her and then out over the small town. "Was wondering if you were ever going to wake," Julian said in a cold tone.

"How long was I out?" she questioned, leaning against the railing.

"Three days, between the fever and the wounds, the doctor said you were lucky," Julian stated.

"Where is Gareth?" she quickly questioned it, then Julian looked at her again and gave a hint of a smile.

"Recruiting," Julian replied.

"Recruiting for what?" Mia questioned.

"The second voyage of the Ulysses will set out in a matter of a couple of weeks." Julian turned to look at her. "And I think this is one journey you will want to take with us."

"Is Gareth going?" she questioned.

"He will be the new head of security. It seems we need someone, a crew of nine… two assassins, two deaths, countless indiscretions. Imagine the trouble of a twenty-man crew," he said as he turned and looked out. "You would be twenty-one if you intend to go with us?"

"Is that an offer?" she questioned.

"A complicated one," he said. "I know of the relationship between you and Gareth. I do not frown upon it even though I called Logan Ezekiel a friend." Mia started to speak, but he said again, "That is why this is almost difficult for me to say. We are going from here to Montana to investigate a second site set up to build an airship like this one." The smile was now gone, and he turned his body to face Mia fully. "It has been over three months since there was a message from the facility. The facility was being run by your husband." He turned his back to her, "There is a letter on the nightstand I believe you will want to read." Julian walked away. She never moved or seemed to blink until he was gone. She turned and looked out; there was a lot of activity below her, and she had a lot to consider. The idea of going out and finding her husband… with Gareth at her side made her heart skip with regret and excitement at the same time. She turned, seeing the envelope on the stand with her name scribbled on the outside, Meghana. She knew immediately who it was from. She smiled as she slowly opened it. Just the sight of Logan's handwriting made her hands shake.

My love, my darling wife.

I've only been away from your arms for a few weeks now, and I can't describe the loneliness I feel. I wish I wasn't writing this… I should already be back on the train coming home to you. To fulfill my promise to you to take you someplace wild. To let you be you…

My friend Hamilton has shown me something marvelous… The future, my wife. He has shown me the future, and I must see where this takes me. I am leaving for Montana in the morning with Alastair and others. Hamilton will, in the coming months, be sending this letter to you, as well as travel arrangements for you to join me. I can't wait to show you what is happening... I've been given the chance to shape the world itself. Only such a grand opportunity would keep me from your arms. Your lips. Now, each night we are apart, I will look up at the stars and think of you. I am sorry, my beautiful wife. We will be reunited one day soon. Until then, I will hold you in my heart.

I love you, Meghana Ezekiel.

Logan.

About the Author:

Steven Paul Watson is many things: a writer, artist, amateur photographer, and avid outdoorsman as well as an all-around geek. His love of writing includes soul-chilling science fiction, fantasy, all things supernatural/horror, and a passion for steampunk/alternate reality.

In his free time spends a lot of time out in nature hiking the hills near his home. There is no better way to stroke one's imagination than being outdoors in the wilderness having real adventures that feed the ones he puts on a page. Steven is also an avid crafter and artist making a lot of jewelry and woodcrafts. Loves dogs and spending time with his family.

Steven Paul Watson

Works By Steven Paul Watson

Fairywood Falls
Widows Ridge

Ulysses Series:
Feather in a Gaslamp

Howling Moon Series:
Howling Moon: The Beginning
Full Wolf Moon

Other Works:

Human 76
(Anthology Entry "The Hunted")